ADAM

Seven Sons Book 1

KIRSTEN OSBOURNE

Copyright © 2017 by Kirsten Osbourne

Unlimited Dreams Publishing

All rights reserved.

Cover design by Erin Dameron Hill/ EDH Graphics

No part of this book may be reproduced in any form or by any electronic or mechanical means including information storage and retrieval systems, without permission in writing from the author. The only exception is by a reviewer, who may quote short excerpts in a review.

This book is a work of fiction. Names, characters, places, and incidents either are products of the author's imagination or are used fictitiously. Any resemblance to actual persons, living or dead, events, or locales is entirely coincidental.

Kirsten Osbourne

Visit my website at www.kirstenandmorganna.com

Printed in the United States of America

Chapter One

Adam McClain sat down across from the new boy coming to live at the boys' ranch. He could feel the anger flowing toward him from his young charge. He glanced at his "cheat sheet" for the boy's name. Ah, there it was. Nicholas.

"Welcome to the ranch."

Nicholas slumped down in his chair, a look of anger filling his face. Adam felt the fury hit him in the face like a ball of pure energy. "I don't want to be here."

"Few boys do…until they've been here for a while and realize what an awesome place they've landed in." Adam gave the boy his complete attention. "Tell me about Nicholas."

"It's Nick."

Adam made a quick note so his brothers wouldn't make the same mistake he had. "All right, then. Tell me about Nick." He sat still, feeling fear coming from Nick. "Start with how old you are and where you're from? There's no need to be afraid of me." As soon as he mentioned being afraid, he felt pride coming from the young man. As an empath, Adam was the counselor at the McClain's Boys' Ranch. Sometimes he loved it, but other times it was hard to feel all the emotions hitting him at once.

"I'm fourteen. I'm from Dallas. I want to go home."

Adam sat back in his chair, steepling his hands under his chin. He'd heard the same words hundreds of times. At thirty-five, he was the oldest of seven children. His mother had a fascination with *Seven Brides for Seven Brothers*, hence the name. His younger brothers were Benjamin, Caleb, Daniel, Ephraim, Frank, and Gideon. They'd been teased about their names a lot, but truth be told, it made him feel like part of a set, which pleased him.

"Do you want to tell me why you're here?" The facts were laid out before Adam. Nicholas had stolen his stepfather's car to go for a joy ride. Add in shoplifting, smoking, drinking, and way too many fights with other boys at school, and his parents had decided to send him away.

Nick shrugged, responding exactly how Adam expected him to. "No one wants me to have fun."

Adam shrugged. "You'll find you're allowed to have fun here. After your schoolwork and chores are done. My name is Adam McClain. You'll come in and talk to me a couple of times a week for a while. We'll become good friends."

"You're a shrink."

"You could say that. I'm a trained youth psychiatrist. The real thing I'm here to do is talk to you about your troubles. We'll start that tomorrow. First, though, I'm going to walk you to your cabin so you can meet the five boys you're going to share a home with." Adam glanced down at Nick's file again. "You'll be starting out in a cabin with two of my brothers—Caleb and Benjamin. You'll be using our first names when you address us, because there are too

Adam

many Mr. McClains to keep up with. We wouldn't know who you were talking to."

The kid didn't meet Adam's eyes. "I'm ready."

"Good. Get your things and we'll go for a little walk." Adam chatted easily with the boy as he walked out of the office and across the ranch with him. "The stables are to your right. You'll be assigned a mount that you will tend while you're here. My brother, Ephraim, is in charge of the stable, and all the other animals here on the ranch."

"A horse?" Nick's eyes brightened, and Adam felt a rush of happiness that was quickly masked. "You don't expect me to start roping cows, do you?"

"That's something you'll learn to do here. You came just a week too late. We had our annual fundraiser over the weekend. We have rides, games, good food, and lots of fun stuff." Adam pointed off to an area that had been trampled by thousands of feet just a couple of days before. "We hold the fundraiser over there."

"Figures I'd miss it." Nick kicked at a clump of grass. "It stinks here."

Adam grinned. "That's the smell of cow manure. You'll get used to it. You might even grow to not mind it so much." The boy would be there for four years. His parents had written him off and completely given up custody of him. "While you're here, you'll learn to work with the cattle, ride horses, mend fences, and generally work hard. You'll go to school every day, and when you get home, you'll work around the ranch. It's a good life."

"Did you get sent here when you were a boy?" Nick asked, seeming to like the idea of the man beside him having had to go to a boys' ranch as well.

"Nope. I've lived here since I was born. I refer to a lot of men as my brothers, because they were raised here along with me. I am the oldest of seven brothers by birth, but there are at least a hundred men I refer to as brother."

"I'm not going to call any of the boys here my brothers. They're just random idiots I'm being forced to live with." Nick looked at everything around him, soaking up the ranch. Adam could feel the excitement radiating off of him.

Adam grinned. He knew the boy would feel differently soon. He stopped in front of a cabin. In truth, the building was more of a house. There were four bedrooms. His brothers shared one, and each of the boys shared with one other. "This will be your home for a while."

Nick wrinkled his nose. "Do I have to share a room?"

"Yup. You'll share a room with Hunter. He's fourteen, and he came here from San Antonio." Adam strode toward the back of the house, opening a door. "This will be your room. Hunter was here first, so he gets his choice of beds. Looks like he's in the one on the left. I'll get you some linens and stay here with you while you make your bed and unpack."

"Make my bed? There's not someone here who can do that for me?"

Adam pulled out a chair that was in front of one of the desks in the room. The furniture was comfortable, but not fancy. There were two twin beds, two chests of drawers, and two desks with chairs. Nothing else. "You'll find that here on the ranch, you will be required to take care of yourself."

"What does that mean?"

Adam had dealt with many boys like Nicholas in the years he'd been working on the ranch. "It means you will make your own bed every day. You will do your own dishes. You'll be expected to take a turn at cooking. Your mother doesn't live here, Nick. You are responsible for you."

Nick frowned. "I'll leave."

Even as he said the words, Adam felt fear wash over him. "You won't leave. You'll love it here. It's just going to take a little while."

"No one can make me love it."

But Nick felt hope, and Adam knew it. "No, no one can make you love it. You'll have to do that yourself. I promise though, if you'll give us a chance, you will love it. I would be willing to bet money that in a year, you'll love this place more than you ever loved living in Dallas."

Nick sat down on his bed, a frown on his face. "No, I won't."

"I've been doing this a long time, Nick. We always succeed in making boys love the ranch. Period." Adam walked to the closet there in the room and opened it, taking down a set of sheets. "Go ahead and make up your bed. I'll stay with you until you're done, and then I'll walk you down to your housemates."

Nick glared at Adam, obviously not wanting to follow instructions, but he stood and took the sheets. As he struggled to put the sheets on his bed, Adam gave light tips. "Make sure you put it over both of the corners at the top before you move on to the bottom. That's right. Good job."

When the bed was made, Nick looked at Adam with pride. He'd obviously never made a bed before, but he did it right the first try. "It's done."

"Yes, it is. Good job. Now put your clothes away." Adam pointed to one of the chests. "That one is yours. Get your stuff in it." He sat down again, waiting for the boy to do as instructed. Always on one of the first few days, the new boys would try to make a run for it. Or they would flat refuse to do something. Nick was younger than most of the boys who came to the ranch, so Adam hoped he'd do what was right.

Nick picked up his things and slowly put them into the drawers. He hadn't brought much, which didn't surprise Adam. They relied on donations from the church in town for clothes for the boys. Usually what the boys brought wasn't particularly suited to ranch life, so their wardrobe was slowly changed anyway.

When he'd finished, Adam led him out of the cabin and toward the hay field. This month was the month Benjamin and Caleb had this particular group of boys, so they were working in the field, adding fertilizer to make it ready for planting again in the spring. Benjamin had the power to make plants grow at a tremendous speed.

Adam and his brothers were the seven sons of a seventh son. Each generation, the seventh son had some sort of power, but this generation was the seventh. And each seventh generation brought a group of men who each had a power. Gideon had every power his brothers had, but all were to a lesser degree.

Caleb's power was sensing danger, so it was always good to start the new boys with him. It didn't always work out that way, but Adam was pleased when it did.

"Your housemates are working on fertilizing the hay field. You'll be joining them. I told you my brothers Benjamin and Caleb will be your house leaders for this month and next. The leaders shift out every two months, so you get to learn skills from each of us."

"What about you?"

Adam shrugged. "I'm the oldest, so I stay in the big house where my parents still live." Truly, he couldn't spend a night amongst the boys. They'd tried it at one point, but the angsty emotions of the teenage years had been too much for his empathic powers.

"That's dumb."

"Why is that dumb? I also have a degree in psychiatry, so I'm a doctor. That affords me special privileges."

"None of your brothers are doctors?"

"Actually, both Daniel and Ephraim are. Daniel's the fourth brother. He's a regular old fashioned general practitioner. Then There's Ephraim. He's the third to the youngest. He's a veterinarian."

"An animal doctor?" Nick shrugged. "Animal doctors aren't the same as people doctors."

"No, they're not. But they're every bit as important." Adam felt the excitement from the boy. "Do you like animals?"

"I don't know. I never had one."

"You've never had a pet?" Adam asked, not at all surprised. "The cat just had kittens. Do you want to claim one?"

Nick looked at him with shock in his eyes. "You'd let me do that? I'm a troublemaker."

Adam shook his head. "You used to be a troublemaker. Now you're going to be a productive, working member of our ranch. You'll see. I'll take you to pick one out when you come to see me tomorrow."

"Why am I getting my head shrunk so much?"

"Because you're new here, and I need to get to know you." Adam stopped when they were within earshot of his brothers. "It's not something to be ashamed of here. All the boys see me every day for their first week. And then gradually less. I see every boy on the ranch at least once a week."

"How many boys are here?"

"Right now we have thirty. We're at maximum capacity

with you. We had room because one of our recent graduates moved out last month." Adam raised a hand to signal Caleb, who hurried over. "Caleb, this is Nick. He's here from Dallas. He's going to share a room with Hunter. He's made up his bed and put his things away."

The boys who were working at shoveling manure onto the field from a wheel barrow all stopped, looking at them. "Hey, Adam!" Jose yelled. Jose was sixteen, and a permanent resident of the ranch. His parents had sent him there when they'd found out about his drug abuse.

Adam raised a hand in greeting. "How's it going?"

"Good! I made a hundred on my history test today!"

"Great job!" Adam was proud of how far Jose had come since he'd been left there two years before. He took a personal interest in every one of the boys, and they took an interest in him as well.

Caleb grinned at Nick. "Welcome to the ranch. We're glad to have you."

Nick wrinkled his nose. "So I can help shovel bull sh—err…poop?"

"Yup. We need the help getting this field ready for spring. Benjamin says cow poop is the absolute best fertilizer there is, and no one knows as much about growing plants as Benjamin does."

"Whatever."

Benjamin waved Nick and Adam over. "We're spreading the manure today." They had a manure spreader, but they preferred to teach the boys how to do hard work, rather than letting machines do it.

Nick walked over to Benjamin, who towered over him by half a foot. "I didn't bring a shovel."

"That's all right. You can use mine." Benjamin handed the boy his shovel and instructed him on the best place to start working.

Adam

Nick moved toward the other boys with trepidation. Hunter hurried toward him. "You're going to share a room with me. I know because all the other beds are full. You'll love it here. It takes a little time to get used to it, but you'll always be treated with respect and love."

Nick shrugged. "Whatever."

Adam stayed with his brothers. "I emailed you both the case history. He was sent here after stealing a car. He's got shoplifting, fighting, drugs, and drinking on his record. His parents have completely washed their hands of him—signed away rights."

Benjamin frowned. "I hate that for him, but love it for us. We'll get to keep him and mold him into the man he's capable of being." In their lifetimes, they'd never failed to turn a boy at the ranch into a productive member of society.

Caleb looked over at Nick. "I always feel bad for the ones whose parents simply don't want them anymore. If they sent them here for a year to get them acting right and took them back, it might be better for them."

Adam shook his head. "You know it's better if they're left with us until they're grown. Always has been." He felt his pocket vibrate and pulled his phone out. "This is Adam."

"Adam, I need you at the house as soon as you can get here. We have something to discuss." Peter McClain was still the acting head of the ranch, though the responsibilities were slowly being taken over by his sons.

"I'm on my way, Dad." Adam ended the call and rubbed the back of his neck. "Dad needs me for something. He sounded a bit upset."

"Really?" Caleb asked. Their dad was never upset.

"I might have read between the lines a little," Adam said with a grin. "See you tomorrow. Email me after the boys leave for school to let me know how he does tonight."

"Will do!" Caleb watched as his brother hurried away.

Adam rushed toward the main ranch house. He was tired. It had been a long day. As the person in charge of intake there on the ranch, a day when a new boy arrived was always a busy one. They were registered foster care providers for up to fifty boys at once, though they chose to only take in thirty at a time, so they could give each individual attention. They took boys from the ages of twelve to seventeen, but usually they didn't come before fourteen.

When he reached the house, he opened the door, calling, "Dad! I'm back!"

His mother came out of the kitchen, putting her hands on her hips. Lillian McClain didn't stand for loud, boisterous voices in her home. "Adam, you know better!"

"Sorry, Mom. Dad called me back, and it sounded like it was an emergency."

"He's in his office."

"Thanks!" Adam hurried off to his dad's office, hating that his mother still felt the need to scold him. He was thirty-five! He knocked once on his dad's door and then turned the doorknob. "Hey, Dad."

"Adam, sit. I got a call from Lois Rendon this morning. She's decided to retire."

"Retire?" Lois was the woman who organized and ran the fundraiser every year. "Do we need to keep the fundraiser going?"

His dad nodded, scrubbing his face with his hands. "You know as well as I do we don't want people to know where the money really comes from. We need to do the fundraiser so we can keep this ranch going with no suspicion."

"Do you want me to take over the fundraiser?" Adam

couldn't imagine finding the time for that, but he'd do it if he needed to.

"No, you do enough around here. We need to hire someone else. I'm going to contact an employment agency to find someone for us. I do want you to interview, though, because you'll be the person working closest with them."

Adam nodded. In addition to his work counseling the boys, he was in charge of personnel on the ranch. "I'll do that. If you can, get the interviews set for Monday. I can take all day and just interview. Well, except for Nick. The new boy will need me every day for a while, I think."

"That sounds good. I'll do my best."

"Anything else?" Adam asked. His father had the power to catch glimpses of the future. He'd be able to bring in the right person with no problem.

"Not now. Just be sure to watch Nick. I don't think he's going to hurt anyone else, but I worry he might be self-destructive."

"I sensed that in him as well. I'll do everything I can." Adam stood, heading upstairs to shower before dinner.

Chapter Two

Tiffani Simpson drove her little Ford Fiesta the hour and a half from San Antonio to Bagley. She hadn't been super interested in the job someone had pointed out, but she was a firm believer in fate. She'd seen the listing, found out she was being laid off, and read something about the ranch all in one day. It seemed to her she was meant to go to Bagley and work as a fundraising coordinator for the boys' ranch there.

She pulled into the driveway, surprised at the sheer length of it. Parking in front of the main house as she'd been instructed, she got out of the car, taking a minute to smooth her hair. It wasn't every day that she drove an hour and a half for a job interview.

She walked to the house and knocked, waiting nervously for someone to come to the door. When the door opened, it was a middle-aged gentleman with salt-and-pepper hair and blue eyes. The kind of eyes that pierced the soul.

"Hi, I'm Tiffani Simpson. Are you Adam McClain?"

The man smiled, shaking his head. "Adam is my oldest

Adam

son. Come in, and I'll call him over." He led her to a small office. "Can I get you something to drink while you wait?"

"I'd love some ice water. Lots of ice." Tiffani's worst habit was crunching on ice, and she needed to do it more when she was nervous—like today.

"I'll be right back." The door closed behind him, and Tiffani wandered over to the window, looking out at the ranch. Doing a fundraiser here would actually be enjoyable. She believed in what these people were doing, and she loved the idea of helping kids who were in the foster care system.

The door opened behind her, and she turned, smiling as she reached for her ice. Instead, she saw a man with the same eyes as Mr. McClain, but he was a great deal younger. And handsome. Much too handsome for her heart rate.

"I'm Tiffani Simpson."

"Adam McClain. My dad is getting you some ice water. Would you like to sit down?"

Tiffani shook her head. "I'd rather stand for a minute or two. I sat the whole way here."

"Where do you live, Miss Simpson?"

"San Antonio."

"If you were to get the job, would you relocate? Or would you continue to make the drive?"

Tiffani thought about his question for a minute. "I'd relocate if I could find a good place to live."

"We have some cabins for rent here on the ranch, if you'd care to look at them after the interview. We've found that when people begin to work for us, we want them close at hand so they can see how the ranch runs."

"I'd like that." The door opened behind her, and Tiffani accepted the water from his father.

"So what can you tell me about fundraising?"

"I've been a fundraiser for three different non-profit agencies. I read an article about your fundraising event the ranch puts on every year in a magazine, and I love the idea of putting my ideas to work for you."

Adam leaned back in his chair, watching her. "What ideas do you have?"

"I know you do rides, a small rodeo, food, and games as part of your fair. What if you had people make some quilts you could auction off? Or what if you had the boys put on some sort of show?"

"I like the quilt idea. I'm not sure how I'd feel about having the boys perform for money." Adam sensed that her ideas were all coming from her heart. She was very enthusiastic about their cause. "How soon could you start?" His father had told him she was the one to hire, but he'd needed to sense her emotions about the job for himself.

"My last day at my current job is Monday. If you could show me the cabin you have in mind for me, I could start as early as Wednesday. Your fundraiser is only once a year, correct?"

"Yes, but we've worked with the same woman for longer than I've been alive. Hiring someone new and getting them up to speed in time for the fundraiser might be a difficult thing."

"I assure you I'm a quick learner, especially when I feel strongly about something."

Adam got to his feet, offering his hand. "Welcome to the team, Miss Simpson."

Tiffani grinned widely. "Thank you. And please, call me Tiffani."

"You'll need to call me Adam. There are a lot of Mr. McClains running around this ranch."

"The article I read said that you have six brothers. I can't imagine coming from a family of that size."

Adam

"How many siblings do you have?" Adam started walking toward the door, determined to give her the ranch tour.

"None. My father died when I was two, and my mother never remarried. I always loved the idea of a big family."

Adam frowned. Maybe he should introduce her to Gideon and forget all about his attraction to her. Gideon was guaranteed to have seven sons. He would probably have several, but there were no guarantees with him. Of course, he could provide her with daughters, and his brother couldn't.

As they walked across the ranch, he pointed out the stables, the barn, the fields, and the boys' houses. He stopped in front of a small cabin. "This is the house we have that you could rent." He opened the door and led her inside. The cabin had originally been built more than a hundred years before by the boys who were the first foster kids there. It had been updated through the years to include electricity and indoor plumbing, but it still wasn't the most luxurious place on earth.

"It's certainly rustic."

He laughed. "It is. You'll find it has all the modern conveniences, though. All the appliances are included, and there's a hot tub at the main house you'd be welcome to use."

"A hot tub? Sold!"

He smiled. "It'll be nice to have you on board, Tiffani."

"I'll be back on Tuesday with all my things. I don't have a lot, so it shouldn't be a big deal to move in."

"If you'll give me a call about thirty minutes before you arrive, I'll arrange for you to have help unloading your vehicle." Adam leaned against the doorjamb studying her. "Will you move alone?"

"If you're asking if I have anyone I live with the answer is no. I'm too married to my job to be in a relationship, I'm afraid."

"I hope you'll put just as much enthusiasm and love into working here at the ranch, then."

Tiffani smiled. "I don't seem to know any other way to be. It's one hundred percent or nothing in my world."

"That's what we need around here." Adam opened the door and led her outside. "I'll walk you to your car."

"Thank you! I'm not sure I could find it at this point."

He grinned. "Let's stop by my office, and I can give you a map of the property. You'll be all over it." He eyed her skirt and heels. "I hope you own some good old-fashioned cowboy boots. Wearing that will just get your clothes ruined."

"I'll be sure to wear something more appropriate when I work here." Tiffani looked at him, a little worried about how attracted she was to this man. He'd be her boss, and office romances never ended well.

Adam felt the wave of attraction come from her and hid a smile. He felt the same. "When you get here, I'll show you around town. There's a church in Bagley that has acted as our benefactors for years. You'll need to be introduced to the pastor and his staff."

"Are you asking me out, Adam?"

"Would you go if I said yes?"

She laughed softly. "Not yet, but give me a little while to get my bearings. Then I just might do it." As much as she was against dating someone she worked with, there was something special about him. She couldn't pass up the opportunity to get to know him better. His eyes—the exact same as his father's—sent her pulse racing. Yes, getting to know Adam McClain was an exciting and scary prospect all in one.

Adam

Tiffani was there by late Tuesday afternoon. She called thirty minutes before she reached the ranch as promised. She drove slowly through the grounds, following the map Adam had given her. When she found the house she'd agreed to rent, she found thirty boys waiting out front for her.

She slipped from her car, surprised. "What are all of you doing here?"

"We're going to unpack your truck for you." The boy who answered looked about seventeen, and he had a big grin on his face.

She'd borrowed a pick-up truck from a friend. She'd take it back the next weekend. "I'll sure let you. I don't exactly love lugging boxes." She was exhausted. She'd finished up at her other job, packing boxes every night. It was a good thing she didn't have a lot to move.

"Start carrying them in, boys. Tiffani, if you would go inside and direct them where to take each box, that would be a huge help." Adam smiled at her as he handed her a key to the door.

She felt a spark rush through her body as she looked at his smile. What was it about him that made her heart beat faster? "I'll do that." She took the key and unlocked the door going inside.

For the next twenty minutes, the boys carried in things. She had them put them in various rooms. The cabin was furnished, so she'd been able to just bring her boxes of stuff.

When they'd brought in the last box, she thanked them all profusely, shutting the door as they left. She leaned back against the door with an exhausted sigh, only to find Adam standing in her house looking at her. "I thought you'd gone."

"Obviously. You look tired. Why don't I stay and help you unpack?"

For a moment, she was tempted, but she really wanted to put everything where she wanted it. She'd shared a house with a friend in San Antonio, but all the furnishings and everything had belonged to the friend. She'd had no say in how things were set up. Here she had every right to move anything she wanted.

"I'm probably just going to unpack the essentials and go to sleep. I'll do a little every night until I'm done."

"You're invited to the house for supper tonight if you're interested."

She wanted to say no, because she really was tired, but she couldn't turn down the invitation. She knew his parents lived in the main house, and telling them no could be career suicide. "I'd like that."

He grinned at her, making her stomach flutter wildly. "Be there at six, then."

Tiffani glanced at the clock and saw that it was after five. She would have just enough time to shower and walk to the house. "I'll be there. Thank you for inviting me."

"You'll have to thank my mother. I was just passing along the invitation."

"I'll do that, then." She stood there awkwardly for a moment. "I need a shower if I'm going to meet your mother."

He nodded, heading for the door. "I need to check in on one of the boys before dinner anyway."

"What exactly do you do here, Adam?"

"I manage the ranch, and I'm the counselor for the boys. If they have any kind of trouble, they always run to me."

Adam

She thought about his words while she showered. She'd read that one of the men was a psychiatrist, and she was more than a little intimidated by the idea of it being Adam. Why psychiatrists intimidated her, she didn't know...but the idea of Adam being one really did.

She got to the house just before six and knocked on the door, hiding her yawn behind her hand. A middle-aged woman came to the door, smiling broadly. "You must be Tiffani. Welcome to the family!"

Tiffani did her best not to react to the strange words. She was working there. Did they consider that made her part of the family? "Thank you, Mrs. McClain."

"Oh, with all the McClains on this ranch and in town, you really need to use my first name. I'm Lillian."

"It's nice to meet you, Lillian. You have a beautiful home."

She smiled. "It's been in the family for hundreds of years. Members of my husband's family fought and died in the Texas Revolution."

"That's fascinating."

"Oh, that's not even the tip of the iceberg with this family. I have a feeling you're going to love it here. Are you settling in all right?" Lillian led her to the dining room where everything was already on the table for supper.

"I am. That little cabin is just the right size for me. I think I'm going to like it here a great deal."

Adam stepped in from another room. "I'm glad to hear that. We like the idea of you staying for as long as possible." When his eyes met hers, she felt a shudder run through her body. He had the bluest eyes she'd ever seen. There was something absolutely mesmerizing about them.

"Thank you, Adam." Tiffani tore her eyes from his and looked at the food on the table. It was a traditional Tex-

Mex meal, complete with enchiladas, tacos, refried beans, and rice. "Everything looks delicious, Lillian."

"Oh, trust me, it is. Mom makes the best food ever. When I was away for college, I'd drive home every weekend just so she could feed me. And she'd always send home frozen meals so I'd have something to sustain myself during the weeks."

Lillian rolled her eyes at that. "He went to UT in Austin. He could have commuted, but he chose to stay in the dorms."

Tiffani grinned at the byplay. It was obvious they were a very tight-knit family. "Well, I can't wait to sample your cooking, then."

Adam's father stepped into the room then. "Hello again, Tiffani. I'm glad you decided to join us for supper. This will be a bit of a working meal, as we will be discussing ideas for the fundraiser next year. We have almost a full year, but you'll need to be working toward it that whole time. We put on a big event so we have enough funds for the following year."

"Sounds good to me, sir." She couldn't bring herself to use his first name, even if she'd known it. It would have been nice if someone had shared that with her. She knew all seven of the sons were named after the Seven Brides for Seven Brothers characters, because that was in the article she'd read.

"Please, call me Peter. Sir will just confuse everyone."

"I'll try my hardest, sir."

They all laughed at her words. Adam winked at her, letting her know that humor was not only tolerated, it was expected. Good. She'd fit right in here.

"Where do you want me to sit, Lillian?" The table was long, and four seats were set at one end of the table.

"Peter will sit at the head of the table, let's have Adam

Adam

sit on his right and you sit across from Adam. I'll sit next to you." Lillian's green eyes sparkled. Adam seemed to be a blend of his parents. He had his mother's nose, but his father's eye color. The shape of his eyes was his mother. He had her dark chestnut hair. His father's strong jawline.

Tiffani took the seat Lillian had indicated. Once they were all sitting, Tiffani was astonished when they bowed their heads to pray automatically. It was definitely not something they did for guests. They prayed before every meal. It was refreshing in this world.

After the prayer, they passed dishes around and filled their plates. There was no doubt in her mind that eating was as serious around here as praying was. Once their plates were filled and she'd had her first bite of the enchiladas, the questions started.

"Have you had a chance to see the place we put the carnival every year?" Lillian asked. "I bake pies for it. A lot of ladies at the church make cakes, and we do a cake walk. There's so much that goes into it."

Tiffani nodded. "I have looked at it. And I have a couple of ideas, if I may."

"Oh, yes, absolutely!"

"Do you know of anyone who would make a quilt that we could use to raffle off? That's something that could be done every month of the year, or you could have several for raffle at the carnival."

Lillian smiled. "I make quilts myself. And many of my sisters-in-law do as well. Anytime a baby is born, we'll make a quilt for them. Maybe the seven of us could sit down and just make quilts for a couple of hours a week. It will force us to get together more often, and we all enjoy our time together."

"You were one of seven children as well, sir?" Tiffani asked Peter.

"I was. I have six brothers. I'm the seventh son of a seventh son. We don't know how far back that goes, but it's centuries. I've tried to trace it further, but genealogy is not my forte." Peter smiled at the shock on her face.

"That's supposed to be lucky or something, isn't it?"

Adam nodded. "Seventh sons are always supposed to be lucky. Unfortunately, I'm just the first son of a seventh son."

Tiffani sat and listened as they told her tales about the family's history. She was utterly fascinated. She'd never heard of a family like this. And she'd grown up in San Antonio. It was surprising word of them hadn't reached her.

Chapter Three

After dinner was finished, Adam looked over at Tiffani. "I'd love to walk you home, if you don't mind."

Tiffani got to her feet. "That would be lovely. Would you like me to help with the dishes first, Lillian?"

"Absolutely not! You go have fun with Adam. I know you're still unpacking. I can handle the dishes…you go work on your house. You should have Adam help you unpack. He's good at that."

"He is? Have you moved often?" Tiffani was under the impression he'd grown up in that house.

"Only for college and medical school." Adam walked toward the door, opening it for her.

He must really be the psychiatrist she'd read about. She had hoped she was wrong. "A doctor?"

"I'm a psychiatrist. My main purpose is to counsel the boys, and I also run the ranch. Dad still has his hands in, but just a bit. Most of it falls on my shoulders now." Adam wanted to reach for her hand as they walked, but he knew she didn't have the advantage of knowing they'd marry someday, like he did. His father's visions of the future had always been more than a little helpful.

"I see. Did your mom ever help run the ranch?"

"I understand she did before I was born, but she had seven boys in seven years. She stayed home and took care of us. Her beliefs were that it was important for a mother to be with her children."

"And you have the whole *Seven Brides for Seven Brothers* thing happening with your names. I know I read that somewhere."

"Yeah, well…my mother has always had a thing for that movie. I've seen it hundreds of times because of her obsession with it. When she married Dad, she knew she'd do the whole seven sons thing, because it's what my family has done for generation upon generation. No girls, just boys. So anyway, she figured if she was going to have seven sons, she might as well pay homage to her favorite movie. So we're named after the brothers from the movie."

"Did she really name one of you Frankincense?"

"No, she didn't, but we still call him that anyway. It makes him crazy." Adam shrugged. "I can't count the number of times he's clobbered Gideon for calling him that."

"Gideon? Why only Gideon?"

"Gideon was the only one smaller than him, because he was the second youngest. I used to slip Gideon a five-dollar bill and tell him to call Frank Frankincense whenever I was annoyed and wanted to see a fight. Brothers do these things."

She laughed softly, shaking her head. "And you were here on a boys' ranch doing all that. Did your parents ever think of making you live with the riff raff?"

He frowned. "I know you're joking, but please don't

Adam

call our boys that again. We treat them as if they were members of the family. Mom actually ended up raising eight boys in our house. There was a Kevin mixed in."

"How did that happen?" Tiffani asked with a frown. Why hadn't she read about Kevin?

"Kevin was left on our doorstep. He had a note pinned to him that named him Kevin, but that was it. He grew up in the house with us, because he came as an infant. Mom never legally adopted him, because she didn't want it to bother the other boys on the ranch that they weren't legally adopted." He shrugged. "I don't know that it would have been a problem, but Mom has always had a lot of empathy. Not as much as me, but she has a lot."

"What does that mean? You consider yourself empathic?"

Adam considered his words carefully. He knew she was safe to know the family secret because they'd marry someday. But was it too soon? "I am empathic. I need to tell you a little more about my family."

She gave him an odd look. They'd reached her cabin. "Do you want to come in for a glass of water? We can discuss it now."

"I'd really like that." He opened the door, going in and sitting on the sofa there in the cabin, waiting for her to bring the water, and thinking hard about exactly how he wanted to explain all this to her.

She came back, handed him the water, and took a seat beside him on the couch, making sure to leave an entire couch cushion between them. She was very interested in him, but he was her boss. How she was going to keep herself in line while she worked for him, she had no idea.

"Tell me about your family!"

"Well, you know about the whole seven sons for the seventh son in every generation. The first six boys don't have to worry about having seven sons, but the youngest does. Every seventh son has some sort of…I don't know exactly how to explain it. Highly developed sense? Anyway, my dad has the ability to see visions of the future. Just little snapshots. He can't control them, though."

"That's fascinating. But the other sons don't have that?"

"Not usually. Here's the deal though…we're the seventh generation. Every seventh generation, all of the brothers have it. So my brothers and I all have slight powers."

Tiffani blinked at him for a moment. "And your power is empathy?"

Adam nodded. "It is. I can feel the disbelief washing off you now." He reached over and took her hand. "I know it's hard to believe, but it's true. We all have something special. Benjamin can make plants grow. He just holds his hand over a plant and it grows before your eyes. Caleb has a sixth sense for danger. He always knows if one of the boys is about to get himself in trouble."

She shook her head. "People told me your family was weird. I see why now."

"Because we really believe this stuff?" He sighed. "You'll see it. Do you want to hear the rest?"

She nodded despite herself. "Yes, tell me them all."

"Daniel has the ability to heal. He can put his hand over a cut or a bruise to heal it. Now he doesn't have the ability to cure cancer or anything like that, but he can do minor healings. And he can take the pain of something away." He could feel the disbelief rolling off of her, but it was all right. She'd see in time. "Ephraim is our animal whisperer. He can communicate with most animals. We realized that was his ability when a rattle snake rose to strike him and he made eye contact with the snake and it slithered away. He was only three at the time."

"Why haven't you been studied? If this is all real—and I'm still not sure that I believe it—wouldn't the universities be sending people out to study you?"

Adam shook his head. "We don't tell people about it. Even our former fundraising coordinator didn't know, and she worked for the family for fifty years."

"Why are you telling me, then?"

He shrugged, looking away. "Dad told me you were safe." He couldn't tell her yet that they were destined to marry. Nothing would freak a girl out more than that.

"What about Frank?"

"Frank has the ability to calm others. He can send out an aura—that's not scientific, but it's the best way to explain it—and all the boys in his vicinity calm down. You'll find that anytime there's a fight or argument among the boys, he's called in to calm them." Adam watched her again, now that their future wasn't being discussed. He needed her to believe him, but he wasn't sure why. He'd hidden this for so long, and she was the first person he'd ever personally told.

"I could see that being very useful here. And Gideon?"

"Gideon's…special. He has all of the abilities to a lesser degree. I can't live among the boys. All of my brothers team up and run the homes the boys live in. I can't, because I can't sleep at night. I am so barraged with the feelings of teenage angst and hormones that I'm overwhelmed. But Gideon can shut off his empathy, which is something I've always wished I could do."

"He can? I can see where that would be very handy!" Tiffani frowned at him. "I'm starting to believe you. Does that make me as crazy as you are?"

He laughed softly. "None of us are crazy." He looked

down at the hand he still held, running his thumb lightly over the palm. "I'm glad you're at least allowing for the possibility that I'm telling you the truth. It matters a lot to me."

She looked at him, slightly afraid of all he was telling her…and what she was feeling for him. "I bet you were thought of as strange in school."

"Definitely! We're all fourteen months apart, and all of our birthdays are on the seventh. It's just crazy, really. But it's our lives. I never played team sports. I could feel how badly the other team wanted to win, so I'd deliberately throw the game because they obviously wanted it more than we did. But then I'd feel the disappointment and anger from my teammates. It was always better if I just backed away and played tennis or something, where I wasn't quite as close to my opponent."

"Wow. I can't imagine trying to live that way."

Adam shrugged. "It's all I've ever known. In daily life I consider it a handicap, but when I'm working with the boys, it's so much easier to get through to them when I know how they feel."

"I can see that." Her eyes met his. "I can see why you don't want this to get out. People would wonder why you don't just find a way to see the lottery numbers, so you don't have to do the fundraising."

Adam felt a slow blush creep over his face. "We use the money from the fundraising to make sure each boy has a trust fund by the time he leaves the ranch. The money from our lottery winnings pays for the ranch and our survival."

She stared at him with surprise. "Then why do you go to all the trouble of your big fundraising event every year? That makes no sense to me at all."

"It gives the boys something to work toward. Plus it

Adam

gives us a real reason for having the money to raise the boys. Everyone knows that our family is independently wealthy from our cattle baron days, but they don't know we get money all the time from lottery winnings. Dad gets flashes of numbers, and we collect the money from it. We've never had a big win and the publicity that brings, but we often win a couple hundred thousand per year."

"Wow. You've given me a lot to think about." She shook her head. "I'm not sure how to pull this together now."

"It'll come to you. You're free to pick my brain on past events. Mom and Dad will both talk to you. Even talk to the boys. Maybe have them put in suggestions for what they think would work. Most of the boys have been here at least a year, so they've seen the event. They look forward to it all year. They don't know what I've told you today. No one does. Dad told me you were safe to tell, so I have, but I want you to be sure not to share that information with anyone."

"I won't tell anyone. If you need me to sign a confidentiality agreement, I'm more than willing."

"That won't be necessary." Adam got to his feet. "Now, can I help you with your unpacking?"

"I can't ask my boss to help me unpack!" Tiffani looked at him as if he'd lost his mind.

"I don't know why not? I'm more than willing."

"I thought it bothered you to be around people." She didn't understand his limitations, but she wanted to. If he was someone who hurt when he was around others, then she needed to know about it.

"I don't mind being around you." He took a step toward her, knowing as he did it, he was making a mistake. He felt for her emotions, but only excitement came back at him. "I think you're beautiful, Tiffani."

She swallowed hard, looking up at him. The words from *Seven Brides for Seven Brothers* came back to her as she looked at him. "They're all as tall as church steeples." She thought it was Martha who said that, but she wasn't sure. "I…I'm not sure what to say to that. I've never thought of myself as beautiful."

He cupped her face in his hands, looking deeply into her eyes. "Well, you are. I want nothing more than to kiss you."

She blinked up at him, surprised. "But you're my boss…"

"I can understand your worry there. We have no rules in our company about it, though, so it's all good."

"It's not a good idea, though." Even as she said it, she knew she wouldn't stop him if he kissed her. His eyes drew her in…so deeply she wasn't sure she ever wanted out.

He sighed. "I'm not going to take the decision from you. May I kiss you, Tiffani?"

All the reasons she shouldn't rushed through her mind, but she wanted him to kiss her. So badly. She'd waited years for her first kiss, never trusting a man enough to let him that close to her. "Yes." The word was a mere whisper. She knew it was a bad idea, but it was so tempting. It was like she was diabetic and a huge chocolate cake was sitting in front of her calling her name.

Adam took a step closer to her and tilted her face up for his kiss. His lips just brushed hers briefly, just enough to make her tingle from head to toe.

"That was a very bad idea," Adam told her stepping back. He felt her emotions as well as his own, and he walked toward the door, feeling like he'd never be able to take his hands from her again. He felt her sadness following him, but he couldn't stop. Not without grabbing her and never letting her go. "I'll see you tomorrow."

Adam

Tiffani grabbed hold of the chair in front of her, doing her best to keep from wobbling. Her knees were weak. He was something else. But why had he run from her?

She sank down onto the couch and buried her face in her hands. Whatever was happening with him, he couldn't blow hot and cold that way. It was messing with her mind.

After a while, she stood up and set herself to unpacking her things. She at least needed her clothes hanging in the closet before morning. And her coffee pot. She was going to need a lot of coffee in the morning.

She went to the freezer when she was done with those two tasks, getting herself a cup of ice to sit and chew, and then she sat down. She picked up her phone and treated herself to one of her favorite shows on Netflix. Sometimes watching the next episode in your current series made all the difference in the world.

———

ADAM WAITED until he was out of eyesight of the cabin and slumped against a building. What had possessed him to kiss her before she knew they were meant to marry? He couldn't just tell her that the combination of their emotions was so powerful he could think of nothing but her. He had to get himself under control if he was going to work with her.

Of course he didn't care about working with her at all. It would be good to have the fundraising in the family, but as far as he was concerned, she'd moved to the ranch to be his wife. He just had to figure out how to convince *her* of that.

He'd always been a strong Christian, and he didn't think premarital sex was good. Tonight was the first time he'd ever been even tempted. He had his morals, and he knew where he stood on just about everything. Never before had emotions rushed through him so hard, forcing him to think beyond his morals. He'd had to get out of there to keep something from happening.

He almost understood why they used to use chaperones. Maybe he should have one of the boys always tagging along when he saw her. If she'd ever see him again. He was going to have to explain just how powerfully their emotions had run through him, and pray his hardest that she'd understand why he'd run. What red-blooded man in this day and age didn't give in to his emotions?

He took a deep breath and straightened up, heading back up to the ranch house. He had to get himself under control so he could sleep. Maybe his mother would have a homemade sleep remedy if he begged. She usually had some warm milk or chamomile tea up her sleeve when he was having trouble settling down.

He got to the house as she was heading up the stairs to bed. Lillian took one look at his face and hurried down the stairs. "Are you all right?"

Adam nodded. "She's definitely the one I'm meant to marry."

Lillian smiled. "I think I understand. Let me get you some warm milk. Do you want to talk? I can get your father."

He shook his head. "No, I don't think I can talk about it at the moment." Sitting at the dining room table, he stared off into space for a moment, while waiting for the milk.

Lillian set the mug of warm milk in front of him. "I'll see you in the morning. Sleep well." She stroked his hair from his face. "I've been looking forward to the day you'd fall in love since the moment you were born."

"I don't know if it's love yet, but it's coming."

"Love rarely comes first for a man. Goodnight."

He drank his warm milk, willing it to do the trick. He couldn't lie awake thinking about her all night and be productive with her the next day. She was his responsibility, and that's all there was to it.

Chapter Four

Tiffani tossed and turned most of the night. She wasn't used to the bed, and she couldn't stop thinking about Adam and that kiss. The kiss had filled her with joy and longing, but his reaction to it had made her feel worthless and sad. Now she had to figure out how she was going to face him.

She got up and wandered into the kitchen, turning on the coffeepot she'd prepared the night before, and then she took her shower. She loved long, hot showers. After she finished, she fixed her hair and put on a long denim skirt with a pair of cowboy boots. Then she put on a pink-checked blouse. She looked professional enough to work, but she also looked ready to walk around the ranch. She had no idea what this first day would involve, but she knew she wouldn't be sitting in an office the entire day.

After getting ready, she went into the kitchen and poured herself her first big mug full of coffee. She'd drink two or three mugs before she was finished. She sat down at her kitchen table with her coffee. She never ate breakfast, but she couldn't live without coffee.

Adam

Pulling up the ranch's website on her phone, she read everything she could about the family and the organization. And then she started researching the seven brothers. She found rumors about how the family was strange, but nothing anyone could prove. And no one seemed to have figured out the brother's powers.

She made it through three cups of coffee as she researched, thinking about everything that had been written. After lying awake most of the night, she realized that what Adam had told her was true. His family was different. She wasn't sure yet if that scared her or excited her. Either way, she would know soon enough.

As she walked across the ranch toward the small building where Adam's office was, and where her office would be, she tried to give herself a pep talk. "He doesn't hate you. He wanted to kiss you. His reaction was unusual, but nothing about him is like anyone else. Maybe that's how he shows he's interested."

When she got to the office, she opened the door and smiled at the secretary sitting at her desk. "Good morning. I'm Tiffani. I'm going to be the new fundraising coordinator."

"I'm Brittany. It's so good to meet you! I'll show you your office." Brittany, a peppy young girl who didn't seem much older than her late twenties, jumped up and led the way to an office down the hall.

Tiffani could see Adam sitting at his desk in the office across from hers. She sat down behind the desk and powered up her computer. Looking around at the walls, she saw that all the pictures were of the ranch and the past fundraising events they'd had. Opening her desk, she had pencils, paper, and everything else she would need to get started.

"Thanks, Brittany."

"You're welcome. I'm here to help you and Adam. If you have any questions, just ask. I'll make phone calls or file for you. Pretty much anything you need is my responsibility."

As soon as Brittany had disappeared, Adam got up from his desk and walked into Tiffani's office, closing the door behind him. "I need to explain about last night."

Tiffani shrugged. "There's nothing to explain. You kissed me. I liked it. You didn't."

"That's not true." He made himself comfortable in the chair across from hers, his mind racing to find a good way to explain what had happened. "When I kissed you, I felt all my emotions along with yours. I'm used to that, but I'm not used to feeling so much. I'm a Christian, Tiffani. I believe that sex before marriage is wrong…but that one kiss made me doubt my convictions. I had to get out."

She blinked at him a couple of times before feeling the heat rise from her neck all the way up to her hairline. "I see."

"That's why I ran away. I felt *way* too much. I wanted to feel more and more, and I knew that wasn't a good idea."

"I'm…not sure how to respond to that."

He shrugged. "I'm not either. It's definitely outside my realm of experience. But I want to see you outside of work. Soon. Will you go out with me Friday night?"

"I don't know…I don't think we should be alone."

"We won't be. The ranch does a Friday night cookout for all the boys. They have to take turns cooking during the week, but on Fridays, Mom makes a humungous potato salad. She does brownies and other desserts. We buy chips. And we make a huge brisket or we make burgers or hot dogs. The boys love the break from their regular routine, and the food is wonderful."

Adam

"And that's what you want to do? What about s'mores? Does anyone make s'mores?"

He nodded. "I'm not sure what Mom has planned for dessert this Friday, but I'll put a bug in her ear. I'll walk you home after, but I won't come in. Being alone with you really isn't an option for me."

"We're alone now!" Tiffani wasn't sure if he was going to get up and run again.

"Yes, but Brittany is in the outer office, and she could walk past and see us, because I left the door open. Also, I'm in work mode." He shrugged. "I'm going to take you around the ranch today, and show you everything you need to know about. I'm even going to show you the cabins. I've found that sometimes it's good to have pictures of the boys' rooms on the internet as part of our website."

"Can I take pictures of things I think we should include?"

"Absolutely! You can't take pictures of the boys, because they're in foster care, but you can take pictures of the ranch and everything here."

Tiffani nodded. "I can do that."

She was a bit concerned about being alone with him on their walk, but if they were in plain sight of everyone, they should be fine. She had strong feelings for him already. Maybe they were just lust, but they were definitely there.

"Let's go, then." He stood up, opening her door. He walked down the hall and explained what they were doing to Brittany. "If we're needed, send me a text."

"I will. Are you going to just show her the ranch? Or take her into town and introduce her to Pastor Stevens?"

"I didn't think of that. Yeah, I'll introduce her to the pastor and others who work for the church. I'll probably take her to lunch while we're in town. Don't expect us back until about one."

"Will do, bossman."

As they left the building, Tiffani asked about Brittany. "How long as she worked here?"

"She and Gideon went to school together. They dated for a bit, but she thought he was too secretive and broke things off. When she graduated from high school, her parents were killed in a car wreck. She has two younger sisters she has custody of now. Dad offered her this job immediately, and she's worked here since. So, I guess about ten years? Maybe eight? I don't know. Close to that."

"She seems really nice." Tiffani felt her heart going out to the younger girl. She wished she knew how to make everyone's life better.

"Brittany's very good at what she does. She seems to anticipate my every whim. If I want some filing done, she does it before I come into work. It's almost eerie at times."

"I think that's a good secretary. I appreciate you sharing her with me."

"Oh, definitely. I'm good at sharing." He walked toward the boys cabins with her. "We have six of what we call cabins for the boys. They're really houses, but calling them cabins makes them feel more rustic and ranchy."

"Is ranchy a real word?" she asked.

"It is now." He opened the door to the first. "Six boys live in each cabin. There are two house leaders in each home. This is the one where Benjamin and Caleb work."

She thought back to their conversation the day before. "Benjamin's power is he makes things grow, and Caleb is the one who senses when the boys are in danger, right?"

"Right." He led her through the home. "The boys share rooms. We put two boys per room, and try to get boys who are around the same age together. The leaders move houses every two months, but the boys stay put from the day they arrive until they move. We try to make their lives as permanent as possible, even though we all know they're in foster care." He opened one of the doors to a bedroom. "This room is shared by the two youngest boys in this house. My brothers share the master bedroom here."

As he wandered through the house with her, he pointed out different things. "House meetings are held every Saturday in the living room. The boys bring up any concerns they have, they deal with assigning chores, and they do a Bible study with it. We're a Christian family, and we raise the boys to be Christian as well."

She nodded, looking around the area. The house was definitely set up for the purpose of having a group of boys living there. The décor was all very masculine as well. "I bet the boys love it here."

"They all grow to love it. Most hate us when they first arrive. They've been taken from everything they know and everyone they love, and most know they'll live here until they graduate from high school." He shrugged. "Our newest boy, Nick, is still in the 'hating us' stage. We're working with him, but he's not a fan of the place. I'm going to take him to pick out a kitten as soon as he gets home from school."

"A kitten? The boys are allowed to have pets?"

"We actually encourage it. Each boy is assigned a horse they take care of, but if they have a small animal as well, they learn to take care of others. Once you can put another being's needs ahead of your own, it becomes easier to assimilate. You learn to care about people. Not all foster care setups are this way, but we are."

Tiffani nodded, liking his reasoning. "And where will he pick a kitten from? The local shelter?"

"No, we had a barn cat who had kittens. She came in one day already pregnant, so we'll wait until the kittens are weaned and then go get her fixed. I'm letting Nick pick from the four kittens she gave birth to."

"Is there an extra for me?" Tiffani had always wanted a kitten, but her mother had been allergic.

Adam grinned at her. "Absolutely. You need to learn to take care of a pet too."

She laughed. "I think I'll be just fine at taking care of it."

"Come with us then. I'll go get him from his chores around three and take him to the cat. He will pick his favorite, and then he'll have to take it home with him. He's an animal lover. That's how we're going to eventually break through to him. Good kid. He just doesn't know it yet."

"I would love that. Come get me before you leave the office. I want to get pictures of the kittens too."

"Remember he can't be in pictures. We'll go over now so you can get pictures of the kittens…but remember, he gets first pick."

"Of course he does. That makes perfect sense to me." Tiffani would have let him have first pick even if it hadn't already been promised to him. She'd always put her own wants and needs behind those of others. She'd learned from her mother to do so at a young age.

"Good." He left the house, carefully making sure the door was shut tightly behind him. "We rarely lock doors on the ranch, because we want to let the boys know we trust them not to get into each other's stuff."

"That makes sense." As they walked, she noticed how tense he was keeping himself. She wondered what it would be like if he kissed her again, right there on the ranch, and she felt her heart skip a beat as they walked.

Adam

"Stop thinking about that. Please." He kept his eyes facing forward, but she knew exactly what he meant. Her emotions were coming in loud and clear to him.

"I'm sorry, Adam. I didn't do that deliberately."

"I know you didn't. I've never felt this much for someone before, so it's very strange for me. I want to spend all my time kissing you, but we know that's not a good idea after last night."

"No, it's probably not." What was she thinking? She had work to do, and work didn't include making eyes at her boss.

He opened the barn door for her, and she followed him to a stall. There were several cows in the stalls, and she wondered why they weren't with the rest of the herd. "Are these cows sick or something?"

"They're all injured in some way. My brother Ephraim is taking care of them, so they're in the barn all day."

"I haven't met any of your brothers yet."

"Oh, you will. Soon you'll be overrun with us McClains." He looked around for Ephraim, spotting him in with the kittens. "You're about to meet one right now."

Ephraim spotted Adam walking toward them and stood. "Hey, Adam. And you must be Tiffani, our new fundster."

"Fundster?" she asked, confused.

"I like it better than fundraising coordinator. Don't you?"

"I guess I do." She grinned, holding her hand out. "It's nice to meet you."

"You too!" He eyed her for a moment. "You don't happen to want a kitten, do you?"

She laughed softly. "Actually, that's part of why I'm here. I want to get a picture of the kittens, and then I'm going to come back this evening when Nick gets his kitten to pick out one for myself."

"Great!" Ephraim was obviously pleased to be able to place another kitten.

Tiffani knelt in the hay and looked at the four kittens, all curled up sleeping against their mother. "Did they just nurse?"

"Yes, but they all know how to eat cat food too. They prefer to nurse still, because it's comforting for them, but it's time for mama to be fixed."

"Is there a vet in town you'll take her to?"

"There is a vet in town, but I will fix her myself. I have a small surgery here in the barn."

"Really? Are you a veterinarian? Why do I not know that you are doctors? Are any of the rest of you doctors?"

"Daniel's a doctor." Ephraim shrugged. "We have a psychiatrist, a veterinarian, and a medical doctor in the family. Good ways to disguise our gifts."

"Gifts is a good way to put it!" Tiffani grinned over at Adam. "You should call them gifts. Makes them easier to understand."

Adam grinned down at her. "I will call them gifts forevermore."

Ephraim watched the two of them, smiling. "Dad's always right, isn't he?"

"He is." Adam didn't want the conversation to keep going the way it was. "Do you have a favorite kitten?"

"I like the little black and white one. He's so sweet looking. I also like the calico, but not quite as much. If Nick wants the black and white kitten, then I will get the calico, and I'll still be thrilled, because I'll have a new kitten."

"I'm glad you've decided. It will make things a lot easier when Nick comes down later." Adam held his hand down to help her up. "Do you want to get a picture of the kittens? When they're asleep is the very best time."

"I'm sure they run around like little crazy beasts every chance they get." She stood and used her cell phone to snap a photo of the kittens. Then she took another of Ephraim holding one of the kittens against his chest and talking quietly to it. She was surprised at the love on his face with the animal. "Do you do better with large animals or small? Or does it matter at all?"

"It doesn't matter. They all seem to respond well to me. I don't specialize in either, because I love them all." Ephraim shrugged. "It's my gift."

Adam looked over at her, taking her hand. He didn't like the way she spoke so easily with his brother. "Are you ready? We have a lot more ranch to see today."

"I'm ready. Let's head out." She followed him from the barn, surprised that he was holding her hand, but she said nothing about it.

"Let's go see the fairgrounds. I know that's not really the correct title, but that's what we call the area where we have the fundraiser every year. Makes it easier for everyone involved."

"Sounds good."

Chapter Five

At around eleven, Adam stopped in his tracks, wiping the sweat from his face. Early October was still a very hot time in the hill country of Texas. "I'm ready to give this up for now. I'll finish the tour tomorrow, but I want to take you into town to meet the pastor and his staff. They're the ones who help us with everything."

"How did you get a church sponsorship?" Tiffani asked, walking along beside him to his truck.

He grinned. "We've had a church sponsorship since we took over the boys. It was back in 1912. My great-grandfather and great-grandmother heard of a fire at the orphanage in Bagley, our closest town. My great-grandmother insisted that she had to have all the boys and take them to live with her. The orphanage was run by the church, but they didn't have money to rebuild, so my great-grandfather agreed, even though they knew they'd have seven sons of their own. So the church continued to help sponsor the boys even after they moved here to the ranch. That's how the boys' ranch was born."

Adam

"I think that's amazing. Why was your great-grandmother so determined to take on other people's children?"

"She was an orphan herself. She was adopted by a wonderful older couple when she was in her teens. At least that's how family folklore tells it. I'm not sure how true it all is. I know her name was Penny Sanders, and she loved the boys." He stopped next to his pick-up truck and unlocked the doors.

She slid in, nervous about being alone with him. "How far is it to Bagley?"

"It's a ten-minute drive. You don't have to be nervous around me, Tiffani. I won't ever hurt you."

Tiffani looked at him with surprise. "Using your gift again?"

"I can't shut it off. I wish I could." He drove out of the ranch roads and headed toward Bagley. "We can do our small shopping trips in Bagley. There's not much there, but it's better than nothing. For the big trips, we have to drive to Nowhere."

Tiffani watched around her, trying to memorize the way so she wouldn't have to ask for directions or get help. When he stopped at the church, she realized he hadn't made one turn. The church was on the same highway as the ranch.

"Do they know we're coming?" she asked.

Adam shrugged. "No idea. They know I stop in regularly, though, so it won't be a problem."

Together they headed into the church and went to the pastor's office. Adam knocked, and they heard the call, "Come in!" As soon as they stepped inside, the pastor smiled. "Adam!"

"I brought my new fundraising coordinator to meet you. Of course, Ephraim is calling her our fundster."

The pastor shook his head. "That boy has always been very strange."

"Not my fault!"

"No one said it was." The pastor shook his head at Adam. "I'm Pastor Stevens. It's good to meet you."

"I'm Tiffani Simpson. I understand I'll be working with you at times."

"Yes, you will. Is there anything I can do for you now?"

"I'm wondering if you have any ladies in the church who craft…" Tiffani didn't see a reason to wait to ask for what she wanted for the boys.

The pastor laughed. "Of course we have women who craft. What kind of craft are you looking for?"

"Anything marketable. I'm thinking of having crafts sold at the fundraiser—more than that, they'll also be raffled off, making more money."

The pastor nodded, smiling. "I'll put out the call on Sunday. We have a whole year to prepare, so we can get some good stuff."

"Thank you, Pastor."

"Adam will give you my number. If there's anything at all we can do, we're willing."

As they left, Tiffani was elated. She loved knowing that she had the full backing of this church. "He's so sweet."

"Yes. He baptized me a very long time ago. I have a lot of respect for Pastor Stevens. Everyone here does. He's a good man." He took her elbow and steered her toward a small café there in town. When they walked in, there was a white board with the specials of the day written on it. Chicken fried steak with mashed potatoes and green beans, all smothered in white gravy was the special that day.

They sat themselves at a small corner table that was meant for four. A waitress brought them the menu, smiling. She was an older lady who was chewing gum a mile a minute. "The chicken fried steak is so good today, it'll make you want to kiss the cook."

Adam grinned. "That does it for me, Miss Mae. I want the chicken fried steak."

"And for you?" Miss Mae asked.

"I'll have the same. And to drink I want ice water, with lots and lots of ice." Tiffani was a bit nervous, and her ice chomping habit was about to take over.

Miss Mae nodded. "Will do. Dr. Pepper, Adam?"

"Is my mama the best cook in all of Texas?" Adam's Texas drawl took over when he asked the question.

"Be right back!"

Adam reached across the table and took her hand. "We're not here as boss and employee. We're here as man and woman on a date, so I'm allowed to hold your hand."

"I don't know what to say to that."

"It's God's way of telling you to let me have my way when you don't know what to say."

She sighed at him. "You're going to be a pain in my backside, aren't you, Adam?"

"I aim to please." His blue eyes twinkled at her.

Miss Mae hurried back with their drinks, putting Adam's Dr. Pepper on the table and bringing Tiffani two glasses, one completely filled with ice and the other with mostly ice and a bit of water.

"Thank you."

Miss Mae looked at Adam. "This one has manners. You should keep her."

"I intend to." Adam looked at Tiffani with a grin.

"You can't just tell people in town that you intend to keep me. Are you crazy?" Tiffani asked as soon as Miss Mae had gone.

He shrugged. "The words have been used to describe me on numerous occasions."

She shook her head. "What am I going to do with you?"

"I can make you a list of suggestions, if you'd like."

"Remember you're my boss, please."

"I already told you, I'm not your boss right now. I'm a man taking a woman he's very interested in to lunch. I might not even write this lunch off."

"That would be silly!"

He grinned. "I'm so glad I've chosen a practical woman to spend the rest of my life with."

"You can't say things like that! Someone will hear you and think we're…courting." She was sure the old-fashioned term fit better than dating did when it came to what the two of them were doing together.

"Trust me, Tiffani. We *are* courting."

Miss Mae set their plates in front of them. "Eat up now. I don't want to have to call your mama and tell her you didn't eat."

After she'd left, Adam leaned forward. "She'd do it too! I came here once during the school day, but we had a closed campus. She called my mother and told her I was here, and I was in trouble. I had to wash every window on the ranch before I got my car privileges back. It took me a month!"

"Sounds like you don't want to cross Miss Mae *or* Lillian!" Tiffani cut into her steak and took a big bite. "She's right. This is good enough that I want to kiss the cook. I hope he's handsome!"

Adam glared at her. "Tiffani will not be kissing the cook," he told Miss Mae.

"Well, my husband is cooking today, and he's old enough to be her grandfather, so I think it would be perfectly acceptable."

Adam

Tiffani laughed. "I'll do my best to restrain myself. Tell him that I'm sending him air kisses."

Adam shook his head at her. "Trying to break up a marriage that has been happy for over forty years."

Miss Mae just grinned. "Sometimes the old geezer needs to kiss a young lady to remember what's he got in me." She wandered away with a smile still on her face.

"I like this place," Tiffani said to Adam. "I want to come back often."

"It's a great little town. I went to Bagley High School."

"Thank you for sharing it with me."

"I want to share my entire world with you."

"You're turning into a great big sap. Have you always been this way?"

"I thought women liked romantic men." Adam sighed heavily. "It's like everything I knew about life is totally wrong."

"It's not. I just feel uncomfortable. I appreciate how loving and kind you are, but I don't know that I can believe the sweetness. Not for me. I've only really known you for two days."

"I want to get to know you better. Is that acceptable, milady?"

She grinned, reaching over for his hand and squeezing it, realizing it was the first time she'd voluntarily touched him. "I suppose it will have to be."

On their way back to the ranch, he told her that he'd send her a list of contacts. "I don't think it's a good time to continue our ranch tour. The boys will be getting home from school in a couple of hours, and I need to send in some reports to the state on some of the boys."

"All right. I'd love to have the names and numbers, so I can get everything going. What's my budget for this fundraiser? Can I do it bigger than it's been done before?"

He shrugged. "I think so. We could probably add another fifty percent to your budget. We prefer that most things be donated, of course."

"Well, sure, but if I can put a bit of money into it, and we can add in a hay ride or pony rides…charge a little for them." She frowned. "I'm sorry. My mind is just spinning with ideas. I can't wait to figure it all out."

He parked his truck in the parking lot in front of their offices. "You get straight to work, and so will I. I'll see you around three-thirty, after the bus drops the boys off."

"Do you have your own school bus that brings the boys here?"

He nodded. "We always have. There are enough boys coming straight here that they assign a bus just to us."

"Nice!" She slipped out of the truck and walked toward the building. "I can't wait for our date on Friday."

"Neither can I. I am going to show you a good time in front of thirty boys, my six brothers, and my parents. Should be fun." He winked at her as they separated and went toward their offices.

As she walked past, Brittany called out, "Tiffani, I have a message for you from one of the vendors of the fundraiser. He's not sure he can make it next year, because he's been offered a big contract."

"Which vendor?" Tiffani was sure she could find someone else to do the same job without a problem. She had a year, after all.

"It's the guy who runs the taco truck."

"The taco truck? That would be like the icemaker being down for the event! No way! I'm going to call in every favor I can to get a taco truck here for it. How would we make it without a taco truck? Imagine!" Tiffani hurried into her office and shut the door.

Adam looked at her closed door, then at Brittany. "I

Adam

think she must like tacos."

"You'll have to file that away for future dates."

"Oh, don't worry. I have no problem doing that!" He went into his own office and closed the door, pulling out the folders of the boys that needed reports written. He loved his job, but he sure did hate the paperwork.

Tiffani was on her seventh phone call of the afternoon, trying to arrange for the taco truck for the event when Adam knocked on her door. "Are you ready to go look at kittens?"

She nodded, finishing her call and standing. "Is Nick here?"

"Yes, he is. He's ready to go get his kitten, too."

She got up and hurried around the desk. "Well, let's go get a kitten."

Nick looked at her. "I get first pick."

"Of course you do. You were promised the first pick. I would have given it to you anyway, though."

"Why?"

Tiffani shrugged. "Have you ever heard the saying that it's better to give than to receive?"

"Yeah, but I think it's stupid."

She laughed. "Well, then you can keep thinking so. I really believe it, though. It feels good to do nice things for people."

"Whatever."

Adam met Tiffani's gaze. "That's his favorite word."

"Whatever." Nick didn't realize the irony of him saying it then, but Tiffani had to keep from laughing.

"Do you know which kitten you want?"

Nick shrugged. "Probably the little calico one."

"I like the black and white one."

"Well, I still get first pick."

"I know you do," Tiffani said. "I'll take whichever one you don't."

They reached the barn and Adam opened the door. "Hey, Ephraim! We're here to steal your kittens away."

Ephraim stepped out into the room. He'd been somewhere, but Tiffani couldn't really see where. "Come and choose which ones you want." He looked at Tiffani. "Do you know how to take care of a kitten?"

"I have no idea! I thought I'd google it tonight." She was sure it couldn't be terribly difficult. People had kittens all the time.

"Then you have to listen to my class about kittens while you play with them and decide which one." Ephraim winked at her, making it clear that the class was really for Nick and not for her.

While she and Nick sat on the floor with the kittens and let them crawl all over them, Ephraim went into a lecture on kittens. He talked about what to feed them and how to litter box train them.

"Do you know which one you want, Nick?"

Nick looked undecided. "Well, I like the calico and the black and white. I want both."

Ephraim laughed. "Only one. Each boy can have one pet, and that's it."

Nick frowned. "I'll take the calico then."

As soon as the words were out of his mouth, Tiffani scooped up the black and white kitten, cuddling him under her neck. "You're going home with me. What do you think of that?"

Nick took the calico and cradled it against him. "Can I take him home now?"

Adam nodded, clapping the boy on the back. "I'm

Adam

going to stay with you as you get him acclimated to the house. I'll go home once Benjamin and Caleb arrive."

"Whatever."

Adam looked at Tiffani. "Can you find your way back all right?"

She nodded. "I have the map you made in my pocket. I'll make it home with no problem."

"All right. I'll see you first thing in the morning."

"I'd like that." She'd hoped he'd come over again that evening, but she knew it wasn't wise. Of course, being wise wasn't nearly as fun as listening to her heart.

As she walked home, she cradled the kitten against her. She was going to need a litter box and some kitten food. She could get those in town, she was sure. At least she hoped she could.

She stepped into the house just as Adam caught up with her. "You need kitten food and a litter box. Some cat toys."

"I do. I wasn't sure where to go for them, though. Do they have a pet store in Bagley?"

He shook his head. "We'll have to head into Nowhere."

"We?"

"Someone has to hold the kitten while the other one drives."

She handed him the keys to the truck. "I'll hold the kitten."

"Sounds good." He walked to the truck and slipped behind the wheel, holding his hand out for the kitten while she got into the truck. "When you need the kitten to have shots and get fixed, just take him to Ephraim. He'll handle everything for you right here on the ranch."

"Sounds good to me. That makes it really easy."

"We're pretty self-contained about a whole lot of things. It makes things easier with the sheer number of boys who live here on the ranch." He drove toward Nowhere, knowing the drive like the back of his hand. "Family lore has it that our great-grandparents met in Nowhere. Supposedly he had a vision when he was five that he would marry a seamstress named Penny. So when he found out there was a Penny sewing at the mercantile in Nowhere, he made the drive out there, and he met her. He hired her to make him ten shirts, in a time when men didn't have ten shirts to their names. He wanted her to be thinking of him."

"That's so sweet!"

"Supposedly they were engaged three days later and married within the month. Penny and Tom were the ones who adopted all the boys from the orphan home in Bagley."

"I think it's really neat that you know so much about your family history."

"It's because we have the whole seventh son thing going on. We like to tell the stories of the people who came before us. Tom was a seventh son. Penny had no problem giving birth to seven sons, the youngest of which was my grandfather."

"I really wish I knew that kind of information about my family." She shrugged. She'd never known anyone who knew so much. It was nice to be around someone who was so rooted in his family.

"Maybe you can marry a man who knows that much about his family."

"Are you hinting at something, Adam? We just met!"

"When you meet the one you know you're supposed to marry, it doesn't take long."

She didn't know how to respond to that, so she cuddled her kitten close and watched as the miles flew past them. Nowhere sounded like a good place to be.

Chapter Six

When they reached Nowhere, Tiffani wanted to be the one to run into the Walmart there to grab the kitten things. She handed the kitten to Adam. "Be careful with him! He's just a baby."

The kitten crawled up Adam's shirt and settled under his chin. "I'm perfectly capable of taking care of a kitten."

"All right!" She jumped out of the truck and hurried in, choosing a white litter box and some cat litter. She found Kitten Chow and put a big bag into the cart before picking up a toy mouse. She had a feeling her new baby would like the mouse. As she thought it, she realized she hadn't named him yet.

What to name a cute little kitten? Oreo? Too common... Ding Dong? Too cutesy... Othello? Too long... Maybe Taz? He whirled around a bit like the Tasmanian Devil when he was awake, which wasn't very often.

As she got up to the checkout, the cashier asked, "New kitten?"

"Yes! He's black and white and cute as can be. What do you think of the name Taz?"

"I love it! Good choice. Thank you so much for not naming him Oreo. Everyone I've ever known with a black and white cat called him Oreo."

"I thought about it, but Taz seems to be much sweeter." Tiffani handed the checker her credit card.

After she'd rung her up, the cashier said, "Enjoy your new kitten!"

"Oh, I will. He's my first pet!" Tiffani pushed the cart toward the truck, stopping to put her purchases into the back seat. She slipped into the vehicle. "I'm naming him Taz."

Adam laughed. "While you were gone, he was jumping around like someone had attached springs to his feet. Not even a minute ago, he curled up under my chin again to fall asleep."

She reached over and took the kitten from him. "You really are a little Tasmanian Devil, aren't you?" She stroked his fur, pleased when he purred. "Thanks for driving me here to get his stuff. I don't know what I would have done if you hadn't come to my rescue."

He pulled back onto the highway to head back to the ranch. "Are you unpacking more tonight?"

She nodded. "I need to. I want it done by the weekend. I got my coffee pot and my clothes unpacked last night. I was too tired to do anything else."

"Well, at least you have your priorities straight. The coffee pot does need to be the first thing."

"I agree." She yawned. "What do you usually do in the evenings?"

He shrugged. "I watch some television. Play some computer games. Spend time with my parents."

"Sounds boring."

"It is. What do you usually do in the evenings?"

"I go out ballroom dancing." She kissed the top of the kitten's little head, loving the feel of his soft fur against her skin.

"Really?"

"No, but it sounds more interesting than what I really do, which is watch television, play computer games, and read."

He grinned. "Maybe we should try ballroom dancing together."

"Do you have any idea how to ballroom dance?" Tiffani asked, studying him for a moment. He had to be the most handsome man she'd ever met. She would never get tired of just looking at him.

"None whatsoever. I guess we could take classes together."

"Are you interested in learning to ballroom dance?"

"Only if it pleases you. I find I'm willing to do just about anything to make you happy. Does that make me pathetic?"

She smiled over at him. "Nope. Just sappy."

"Why don't I help you unpack tonight?"

She nodded slowly. "I don't have anything to feed you, though."

"We could hit fast food on the way to the ranch. There's a Taco Bueno on the way."

"Oh, yes! My favorite! I want two tacos and a beef potato burrito."

He grinned over at her. "Did you hear that our taco truck backed out of the event next year?" He knew she'd heard, but he couldn't help teasing her about it.

She nodded. "I've talked to three different taco truck drivers, trying to get them to come. I don't know what we'll do if we can't get someone."

Adam laughed softly. "Maybe you could open your own taco stand."

"Don't think I wouldn't! We have to have tacos if we want to be happy. Tacos mean many happy people!"

"We do a big brisket and lots of barbecue."

"Barbecue is good, because this is Texas, but we also need tacos!" Tiffani was shocked she needed to explain this to him. He was a native Texan as well!

"All right. We'll make sure a taco truck is present."

"I believe that's my job, Adam."

"I know it is." He looked at her for a moment while he waited for the car ahead of him in the drive through to pull forward. "You're beautiful when you're talking tacos."

"They bring out the best in everyone!" She looked down at Taz. "Don't they bring out the best in everyone?" She stared at the cat for a minute. "You know what? I don't think you're a Taz after all. You're a Bob!"

The kitten looked up at her and let out a loud meow. "I think he agrees with you!" Adam told her. "I've never heard of naming a cat Bob before, but it seems to suit him very well."

"Of course it does. He's a Bob!"

"A bobcat?" Adam grinned at her as he waited for her to groan. "I feel like we've been together forever. You're already groaning at my jokes!"

"Together? You think we're together?"

Adam's face grew serious. "I think I want you to be mine. I'd marry you tomorrow if I thought you'd agree and if the state of Texas would agree with it."

"I can't agree to marry someone I don't know well. I just can't. And you have to meet my mother before I can even consider marrying you."

"When will you see her again?"

She waited to answer him while he ordered their food.

"I'll see her this weekend. I'm driving the truck I borrowed back to San Antonio and picking up my car."

"I'll go with you."

She bit her lip. Never in her life had she taken a man home to meet her mother. She just had never met anyone that she was serious enough about to do that. "I don't know…"

"Introducing me to your mother is not the same as agreeing to marry me. I promise. I just want to meet her and get to know her. She's important to you, so she's important to me."

"I don't even know how to respond to that. I've never known a man could be so sweet. I haven't taken a man to meet my mother, so it will be strange…"

"Call her and see if it's okay. I can share the driving with you."

As soon as he picked up the food and paid for it and she had the smell of tacos in her nostrils, she called her mother. "Mom, I'm going to bring Uncle Simon's truck back this weekend. Is it okay if I bring a man home to meet you?"

"A man? What's this man's name? Are you dating him!"

"Yes, I am. His name is Adam."

"Isn't Adam your boss? Tiffani, you can't date a man at work!"

"There's no rule against it." She looked over at Adam, watching him as he drove.

"Bring him, then. I'm praying for you, honey."

"Thanks, Mom. We'll see you on Saturday." Tiffani knew she'd need to call her mother later to clarify.

Adam looked over at her as he pulled into the ranch's driveway. "She doesn't want to meet me?"

"She doesn't think I should date my boss or any man at work. She's praying for me."

"Okay. I'll convince her otherwise." He was going to marry her, and if she wanted to continue doing the fundraising for the boys' ranch it would be up to her. He would hire someone else if she preferred, though. He was marrying her either way. The sooner he convinced her of that, the happier they would all be.

Once he'd parked beside her cabin, he got the bag from the backseat and took the Taco Bueno bag in. He'd never met anyone who got as excited about Taco Bueno as she did, but he didn't tell her that. Many people thought that Taco Bueno was a Texas delicacy.

She opened her door, carrying the kitten. As soon as they were inside, she put the kitten down to let him explore. She set up his food and water bowls before she set up his litter box, and then she washed her hands.

Adam had gotten them each a glass of water, and he'd remembered to get her a separate glass of ice. In that moment, she knew she could love the man. Anyone who would be kind enough to get her a glass of ice was the man she wanted to spend forever with.

She took her tacos and burrito out of the bag. "I haven't unpacked my plates yet, just my mugs and glasses because I needed coffee so badly. Do you mind eating off the wrapper?"

He shrugged. "I'm a guy. We eat off wrappers all the time. No big deal."

"I can't see your mother letting you eat off a wrapper."

"I did spend many years in college and medical school. She has no idea what I did during that time."

"Do you ever wish you could live with the boys like your brothers do?"

He nodded. "I always have envied Gideon. He has the

power of empathy, but he can shut it off. It would be amazing if I could just use it when I wanted to." He frowned at her. "And you don't need to pity me. I've come to grips with it, but I do wish I had more freedom."

"I can understand that." She reached out and covered his hand with hers. "I think you're a really incredible person, by the way. I love that you've chosen a career that works so well with your gift."

"I can't imagine doing anything else. I always knew I wanted to counsel the boys, and I figured I'd just get a degree in psychology and run from there, but I felt prodded to be a psychiatrist. I do love what I do. And I love that if my brother needs help treating people, I can jump in and help."

"Daniel is the doctor, right?" She was starting to have a hard time keeping the brothers straight. So far, she'd only met Ephraim.

"Yup. He's a good man too. If you ever get a minor cut go to him, and he'll fix you immediately. We never take the boys in for stitches, because there's never a need. He can heal them a whole lot faster than the hospital could."

"Broken bones too, right?" She knew he'd told her all about Daniel's powers, but she couldn't remember specifically what he'd said.

"Yes, broken bones too. He just can't heal the huge stuff. Diabetes, cancer, cerebral palsy. Little stuff is easy as pie. If someone is lying on the ground bleeding out, he can at least slow down the blood. He's very good at what he does."

She finished her taco and crumpled the wrapping tossing it toward the trash. She missed, and it landed on the floor, where little Bob pounced on it. The ball of paper was almost bigger than he was, and she laughed when she watched him play with it. "I think I'm going to love having a pet. I'll never be lonely again." She hadn't meant to tell him she'd been lonely, but it just slipped out.

"I'll make sure you're not lonely, Tiffani. You're never getting away from me."

"Well, that sounds very stalkerish. You're not going to stalk me, are you?"

He laughed. "Nope. I'm going to make you the most loved woman alive." He looked at her, realizing then that he was in love with her already. He'd known her for a week and a half, and all he could think about was marrying her. He knew that's how it happened in his family, but he really hadn't ever expected it to happen to him.

She frowned at him. His emotions were so strong, and he was so truthful about them. She was pretty sure she was falling in love with him, but she didn't feel comfortable saying so. What if he thought that meant she would marry him right away?

"I'm going to start unpacking my kitchen. If you want to help, you're welcome to."

He watched her for a moment before nodding. "I'd be happy to help you." He would just have to be sure not to touch her. Being alone with her this way was really bothering him.

He walked to her living room, carefully avoiding watching her, and he began to unpack boxes. There were a lot of book boxes, so he put books on the shelves. "I'm not sure if you want your books in any certain order, but I'm just going to put them wherever. You can rearrange them later."

"Sounds good. I usually alphabetize by author and separate into series and order in the series. I won't ask you to figure all that out for my romances."

"I appreciate that very much!" He had already emptied two boxes onto the first shelf. "You have a lot of books."

He did too, but they tended to be medical books. Hers were all pleasure reading. He found that intrigued him about her. "You must really love to read."

She grinned as she found her plates, carefully stacking them on the shelf in her cabinet. She briefly considered washing them, but she'd packed them carefully, and she'd put them in the boxes clean. "I do. I've been an avid reader since I was a teenager. My mom loved romances, so I started reading them as well."

"My mom reads them, too. I thought they were like girl porn for years, but Mom says they all have stories that end in happily ever after." Adam found it a bit odd that a girl who read romance novels wasn't more receptive to the idea of meeting a man and marrying him a few days later. Maybe she read the wrong romances.

"They are. I don't read the smutty books, though there are a lot out there. I don't look down on women who do read them, either. I figure if they take them out of the real world for a little while, then they're worth reading." Tiffani put away a stack of bowls. "I hate books that don't end in happily ever after, which is why I read romance. I read a young adult recently, and it just broke me. The heroine died at the end of the third book, and I cried for days, and then I got angry. I went through every stage of grief."

He grinned at her. "You get very involved in your books, it sounds like."

"You don't?"

He shrugged. "I haven't really read any fiction since the Harry Potter books. I'm more of a medical journal kind of guy."

She wrinkled her nose. "I can't imagine why anyone would read non-fiction when there are so many wonderful stories in this world."

"Let's agree to disagree there, shall we?"

She nodded. "I guess we can."

At that moment, Bobcat came careening around the corner and crashed into her leg, falling back onto his bum. She laughed softly, happy that he was getting used to his new home. She scooped him up and snuggled him under her chin. "You're a silly kitty, Bob. You really are!"

Adam watched her from across the room, mesmerized by how sweetly she treated the kitten. He could picture her holding his baby. He took a deep breath closing his eyes to remove the vision. She needed time, and he was going to give it to her if it killed him.

At least she was willing to go to the Friday night cookout with him. And she was going to take him home to meet her mom when she'd never taken any other man. He'd have to let that be good enough for now.

"I'm going to head home. I'll see you in the morning?" He wasn't tired yet, and he could stay longer, but he felt his feelings for her building again. With the depth of his emotions, if he got even the slightest inkling that she was thinking about his kiss, he was going to go over the edge.

She nodded. "Sounds good. I'll be right on time!"

"Plan to spend the morning touring the ranch with me again. I'll feed you as well."

"More Taco Bueno?"

He chuckled. "You're a cheap date if Taco Bueno is what you really want." He started toward her to kiss her goodnight, but he stopped himself. "Goodnight, Tiffani. Dream of me."

As she watched him leave, she had a smile on her face. How could she do anything but dream of him? He didn't give her a choice.

She quickly called her mother to explain. "Sorry I couldn't say more earlier. My boss is making a hard play for me, but his parents know, and they seem to approve. It's their company, so it just doesn't feel wrong. Maybe it should, but it doesn't."

Her mother still sounded concerned. "I hope you know what you're getting into. Men can be deceiving."

"I know that. I'm going to be fine, Mom."

"All right. I'll take your word for it."

Tiffani sighed. "I'll see you Saturday for lunch. I love you, Mom."

"Love you too. Take care of yourself."

As she set the phone down, Tiffani frowned. She hoped her mother wasn't right. She didn't want to get hurt.

Chapter Seven

After work on Friday, Tiffani hurried home from the office to get ready for the cookout. Adam was supposed to pick her up at six, which gave her less than an hour to get ready. He'd told her that the meal usually started at six-thirty, but his mother and the boys tended to do all the work for Friday nights.

She changed into jeans and a pink gingham button-up shirt, adding a cowboy hat and her pink cowboy boots. She was just taking a moment to look at herself in the mirror and make sure she looked all right when a knock came at the door.

She scooped the kitten up in her arms, afraid he'd try to get out, before hurrying over to open the door. "Hi, Adam."

He looked her up and down. "You look beautiful."

"Is this outfit all right? I don't want to stick out like a sore thumb."

"You'll find that everyone is dressed pretty much like you are. Of course, no one else will wear it quite like you do!" Adam took her hand and pulled her toward him. "Do you have any idea how much I want to kiss you?"

She shook her head, blushing a bit. "No, but you know how much I want you to kiss me."

He sighed. "Maybe you should be an empath too. It would help you understand my struggles."

She nodded. "We should just go, shouldn't we? Do I need my purse?"

"Nope. You just need you." He took the kitten from her and set him on the floor, taking her hand and pulling her out of her small house. "We're going to do a lot better if we're surrounded by people."

She closed the door and then stopped, looking at him. "But you have a hard time being around a lot of people."

He shrugged. "I do. I managed to make it through both college and medical school with people surrounding me, though. I'm just happier and less stressed with fewer people."

"Do you usually go to this?" she asked, curious about the activity.

"I try to go every week, but it's hard for me. It's perfect for a first date, though, so I think we should do it."

She frowned. "I don't want to make you uncomfortable just because I need to be around people."

"I need to be around people, too. If we're not around a lot of people, we'll have a hard time keeping our hands off each other."

She blushed at his wording, but she knew he was right. His shoulders alone had her drooling, but when she added in his eyes, she really had problems. "Let's go then."

He led her to his truck. "It's done up at the main house, so it'll be easier to take my truck. You're going to be eaten up by mosquitos on the way back otherwise."

She got into the passenger seat of his truck, looking around her. "The ranch is huge. How big is it?"

"Approximately twenty-thousand acres, give or take a few." He knew the number sounded huge to some, but the King Ranch in South Texas was seven-hundred-fifty-thousand acres. His family's spread was downright miniscule in comparison.

"That's so big! How do you run it?"

He grinned. "We have two bunkhouses that each house fifty men. They do the majority of the work. We have the boys split into five work crews, and they're expected to pull their weight. We don't have them here for the free labor, but it helps them to learn work ethic and how to be productive members of society."

"That makes a lot of sense to me. Do you have to pay them for the work they do?"

"We choose to pay them. I'm not sure if we have to, but providing them pocket money helps them to learn to manage money as well. We do a lot of outings, and let the boys get used to having their own money. It's a good learning experience for them."

She nodded. "Why only boys? Were there no girls in the original orphanage?"

"There weren't! So we kept it as a boys' ranch. With my family always having seven sons, we also think it's smart to not have girls running around everywhere. The way it's set up, the boys are perfectly comfortable running around shirtless."

"Makes a whole lot of sense." She really couldn't imagine what it would be like on the ranch if there were girls running around.

He pulled off to the side of the main ranch house, and as she opened the door of the vehicle, she could smell the brisket cooking. "That smells so good!"

Adam

"My mom makes the best brisket in the whole state." He took her hand as they walked toward the people. "Have you met a lot of the boys yet?"

She shook her head. "Just Nick."

"What do you think of Nick?" he asked, his eyes automatically scanning the crowd for the boy.

"I'm not sure. He seemed to almost be disappointed to choose the calico cat because he wanted to thwart me. He just struck me as very unhappy."

"He is. Most of the boys go through that when they first arrive. They think they are here because they aren't wanted anywhere else. They don't understand that for most families, this is a last-ditch effort to turn their kids into productive members of society."

"That's really sad. I feel bad for him."

Adam sighed. "I do too. Sad thing is he really needs to be here. We can help him if he'll let us." He spotted the boy standing with his housemates along with Caleb and Benjamin and immediately headed in that direction. "Hey, Nick! How's it going?"

"I want to go home." Nick wouldn't even meet Adam's eyes as he said it. Adam knew Nick would never go home. Very few boys did once they made it to the ranch. Going home put them back into the same situation they'd been in, with all of the negative things that could happen. No, Nick needed to stay there.

"That's not possible right now. How's the kitten?" Adam deliberately changed the subject to positive things, trying to distract the boy from his desires.

"He's great. I'm calling him Crush."

"I love that name," Tiffani told him. "I named my new kitten Bob. He's a bobcat now."

"That's really bad. Old people humor always makes me wonder." Nick wandered off, but he had a slight smile on his face. He was obviously starting to enjoy himself.

Adam frowned after him. "He's thinking about killing himself."

"What? No way!" Tiffani was shocked. The belligerent boy she'd met didn't seem even a little bit suicidal to her.

"He's doing his best to mask it. Before he came to us, he spent two weeks in a hospital detoxing. He's so used to masking his emotions that he's having a hard time dealing with them all now."

"Is there anything we can do to help him?"

"I'm going to talk to Caleb and Benjamin. We'll put him on a suicide watch. At least for the next month or so. No matter how happy he seems, he'll need to be around someone at all times." He looked down at her for a moment. "Come with me, and I'll introduce you to two more of my brothers."

They made their way through the crowd to two tall men on the other side of the huge fire pit the brisket was roasting on. "Benjamin, Caleb, you both need to meet Tiffani. She's our new fundraising coordinator."

"Oh, the fundster. Ephraim mentioned you!" One of the brothers held his hand out to shake hers. "I'm Caleb."

"It's nice to meet you." Tiffani felt a little shy meeting his entire family this way, but she had to get over that.

The man who must be Benjamin smiled down at her. "So you're going to be the ball and chain, are you?"

Tiffani felt like a deer in the headlights of an oncoming semi. "I wouldn't say that. We only just met."

"But Dad said…" Benjamin frowned at Adam. "She's the one, right?"

Adam shrugged. "Maybe we could talk about this later."

Caleb laughed. "Yeah, like when she's not standing

Adam

right there. Sorry, Tiffani. Our family believes in all these silly gifts of ours."

Adam looked upset. "I need to call a suicide watch on Nick. I'm getting worried about him."

Caleb nodded. "I'm feeling the same stuff. We've been watching him and will continue."

"Good thanks. Now I get to go try and explain things to my girl, because she's standing next to me quietly freaking out. Thanks, guys. You make life so much more interesting."

"Sorry, man." Benjamin said the words, but he looked more amused than sorry. He obviously thought throwing his brother under the bus was fun.

Adam took Tiffani's hand and led her away from everyone to one of the picnic tables that was not yet occupied. "I guess I need to explain."

Tiffani sat down on the bench and looked at him, waiting for a moment. "That would be really nice. I need to know what on earth your brothers were trying not to say."

He sighed. "I told you that Dad has flashes of the future. He told me that you were the one I needed to hire and get to know. He thinks we're destined to marry."

She gaped at him for a moment. "Destined to marry? Do you believe in that hogwash?"

"As a matter of fact, I do believe it. I believe it with everything inside me. So I made sure that I got as close to you as I could as fast as I could. There's nothing against you, but I do believe we'll marry someday."

"Would you have approached me if your father hadn't put that bug in your ear?" She wasn't sure if she should even believe in his interest now. What if he was only doing it because his father thought he should.

"Yes, I would have. I saw you and felt an instant

connection." He sat beside her, taking her hand in his. "I really do believe that my attraction for you is something that would have been there regardless. I've never felt this strongly for anyone in my entire life."

"I can't just date you and marry you because your father has decreed it's going to happen."

"Then date me because you have feelings for me, and know that I'm doing the same. Nothing that I feel has anything to do with what my dad said. It really doesn't."

"That's hard to believe. If it's true, why didn't you tell me what he said to begin with? Then we wouldn't be having this conversation!"

Adam fought for the words to explain. "First off, I didn't know if you'd even believe in destined marriages, and then when you acted like you were starting to believe in my family's powers, I didn't want you to feel forced to date me because of something he'd said. I wanted you to like me for me, not because there was a destiny between us."

She frowned. "I guess that makes sense. I just feel like I've been kept in the dark, and that's very frustrating."

"I know, and I'm sorry." He leaned forward and pressed his lips to her cheek. "I'll try not to keep anything from you again."

"Try not to?"

"I'm a psychiatrist. I can tell you about the boys, because you work here too. If someone comes to me with another kind of issue, I can't just run around blabbing about it. I have to keep things confidential."

Tiffani thought about what he'd said for a moment before nodding. "I can understand that. But if there are any more prophecies concerning me, then I want to know about them immediately."

Adam

Adam nodded. "Absolutely. I wouldn't dream of keeping anything else from you."

"I'm glad." She leaned into him for a moment, thinking about being destined to marry him. If it was true, she would spend forever with him. How strange to think she might be sitting next to the man she would spend her life with.

"Are you angry with me?"

She shrugged. "Not if you're never going to do it again. I never thought to tell you when we started a relationship that if there were any prophecies about us, I needed to know all about them immediately."

"It's just not something you say when you start dating someone, is it?" He grinned, thrilled to have that out of the way. "Do you want to just go ahead and marry me now?"

She laughed. "That's not a proposal. I will not just marry you because your dad has decreed it."

"It was worth a try, wasn't it?"

"No, not at all."

Adam grinned. "I'm one of those guys...give me an inch and I'll take a mile!"

"I see that now."

They were interrupted by a loud whistle from his father. "Gather round for prayer, and then we'll eat!"

After a prayer by the family's patriarch, they all got into a line and served their own food. The excitement around them was palpable. "The boys really like this tradition, don't they?"

Adam nodded. "They love it! This has been going on since before I was born. My grandmother did it when she was alive. She'd make a huge meal for all the boys every Friday night. When my mom took over, she was thrilled to be able to carry on the tradition."

"That's really cool!" She looked over at Lillian, who

was wearing an apron and serving potato salad with a serving spoon. Beside her was Peter, who was cutting off pieces of brisket for everyone.

The spread of food was absolutely amazing. There were fresh baked buns to make the brisket into a sandwich. There were baked beans and a salad. The whole meal looked delicious.

When it was her turn, Tiffani filled her plate. "Thank you for cooking, Lillian. The food smells absolutely delicious."

"It's my job. When you're blessed with a big, wonderful family as I've been, you do what you need to do for the people around you."

When they were seated a few minutes later, one of his brothers and Brittany both joined them. Brittany looked at the other man. "Are you still following me around? You've been doing this since first grade."

"I seem to remember you following me around in kindergarten. Trying to catch the boys and kiss them."

"That was just a phase I went through for a month or two."

"A month or two? You mean nine months. That's long enough to have a baby, little missy!"

"Gideon, you're more than a little crazy."

"Oh! You're Gideon!" Tiffani was thrilled to finally meet the seventh son. "It's so good to meet you. I'm Tiffani."

"You're the girl who's destined to marry Adam!"

"Does everyone but me know this?" Tiffani shook her head with disgust.

Brittany grinned. "No one came right out and told me, but I knew. I've watched you two together."

Adam reached over and squeezed Tiffani's hand. "We are pretty obvious."

"I don't know about that!" Tiffani protested.

Brittany shrugged. "I think you are. But I like to watch people for signs of relationships. I'm a romantic at heart."

Gideon grinned at Brittany. "You want romance? I'll show you romance!"

"You are crazy. You have no interest in me other than flirting. Go away, Gideon. Maybe one of your sane brothers will ask me out."

Gideon attacked his food, but Adam could feel the hurt washing off him. He gave his youngest brother a commiserating smile. "If anyone looks for me tomorrow, I'm driving to San Antonio with Tiffani. Her mother wants to meet me."

"Oh wow! Meeting the mama already? Does Tiffani know what that means?" Gideon asked.

Tiffani wrinkled her nose. "I met his mama on Tuesday, before anything even started between us, so it can't mean that much."

"It does." Gideon winked at Tiffani. "Big brother is awfully interested in you."

After the meal, they all sang a few campfire songs, then made s'mores. Tiffani sat close beside Adam the whole while. Why did she feel so out of place without him beside her, but so comfortable with him there? It was strange just how much she cared about him after such a short time. Maybe his dad was right and they really were destined to marry. She had no way of knowing.

"Is your dad ever wrong about this destiny thing?" she asked, leaning close to him after she'd finished her s'more.

"He never has been. I suppose it's possible that he could be someday in the future, but for now, no he hasn't been." He shrugged. "He knew he was supposed to marry Mom the second they met. He'd had a vision about her."

"Well, that's silly. Is nothing left to chance in your family?"

"A lot is left to chance in my family. But we do believe that you're not complete without your mate. The one you're meant to have, not just any random person. So when Dad has a vision that someone should marry, they actually focus on that person to see if they're right. And they always are."

"Doesn't that take some of the fun out of life?"

"I don't think so. I have a lot of fun, anyway." Adam didn't want her to think her life would be devoid of fun if she married him.

Chapter Eight

By the time the cookout was over and Adam was driving Tiffani back to her home, she was exhausted. It was a good tired, though, that came from a busy week of working hard and unpacking. "I think I'm going to love it here. The ranch already feels like home."

His hand covered hers where it rested on the seat between them. "I'm really glad. Now that I've met you, I can't really imagine letting you go."

She looked over at him, her cheek resting against the back of the seat. "Is that your father's vision talking, or is that you?"

"They're one and the same at this point. I wish I could differentiate." He knew why his father had told him he would be married to her, because it made it so he'd hired her. But he wished he hadn't known.

"Me too." She watched him drive through the ranch toward her little cabin. Her first real home she didn't have to share.

When he'd parked in front of it, he turned to her. "I'm not going to come in tonight."

"I don't recall inviting you," she said, grinning at him.

"I worry about being alone with you when my feelings are so strong." He sighed. "What time should I be here in the morning for our drive to San Antonio?"

"I'd say nine. I need to get the truck back to my uncle, and then we're having lunch with Mom."

"I'll be here then." He opened the door of his truck and got out, surprising her. Hadn't he just said he wasn't going to stay?

She got out and met him next to her front door. "I thought you weren't coming in."

"I'm not. I'm going to be a responsible escort, walk you to your door, and kiss you goodnight." He reached out and removed her cowboy hat. "I can't kiss you if our hats are bumping together."

"So why not remove your hat instead of mine?" Her heart was beating faster at the mere idea of kissing him. How did he affect her senses so much?

"Because I wanted to be able to touch your hair when I kissed you." He stroked a tendril out of her face and behind her shoulder.

"What if I want to touch *your* hair?"

"Are you just trying to be contrary?" He reached up and removed his hat, setting it on the top of his truck. "There, happy now?"

She nodded, her eyes meeting his. "I think I am. But I'll be a lot happier after you kiss me."

"Well, get over here, then!" He caught her by the waist and pulled her close to him, lowering his head to press his lips to hers. His hands stroked over her shoulders, smoothing her hair away from her face.

Her arms went around his neck and she held to him, feeling a tingling deep in her stomach. She could stand there and kiss him all night.

When he pulled back, his eyes were glazed. "Goodnight, Tiffani. I'll see you in the morning."

She watched him get into his truck and drive away, her knees weak. "G'night, Adam," she whispered as his tail lights disappeared.

She went into the house and picked up the kitten, who was meowing at her. Snuggling him to her chest, she walked into her room and sat down at the edge of her bed. "Well, what d'ya think, Bobcat? Am I meant to marry him? Or is his daddy crazy? Or maybe a little of both?" She sighed. Answers would be fabulous.

ADAM WAS THERE ten minutes before nine the following morning. Tiffani had a water bottle in her hand as she shut the door and walked to the driver's seat. "You're not going to let me drive?" he asked, frowning at her.

"Are you one of those macho guys who always thinks he needs to drive everywhere? If so, this does not bode well for our relationship's future."

"Not really. You just look tired, and I thought you'd want to be able to sleep if you got tired along the way."

She handed him the keys without another word. "Are you always so good at talking your way out of trouble?"

"Not at all. I just tell the truth. One thing I learned from a very young age is that if your father has visions, lying is not a good idea. I have never been one to lie as a result."

Five minutes later, they were on the road, heading toward Austin and San Antonio. "Where did you grow up?" he asked.

She shrugged. "Mom and I lived in an apartment complex. We lived in the same one for as long as I can remember. There was never a lot of money, so it was better that way."

"And you went to college, I know. Pell Grant?"

"I had a full Pell and I also had a scholarship. I was valedictorian of my graduating class, so I had a scholarship to any public Texas university. I went to UT San Antonio, because it was close to my mom, and I could see her as often as I wanted."

"And you majored in Business Administration?" He'd read it all on her resumé, but he wanted to hear from her how she'd decided on that as a major.

"Yeah. I started out as an English literature major, certain that I'd spend my entire life writing. It's a lot easier to start a book than it is to finish one, so I started taking some business courses. My senior year I interned for a not-for-profit agency, and I loved it so much that I never stopped working there."

"I think that's great!"

She grinned. "I love it. They were having some issues with the management, and I was laid off from them right before I came here. It worked out perfectly for me."

Adam nodded. "I never would have thought about working for a not-for-profit if my parents hadn't run one my entire life."

"What do your parents do now? Do they still work?"

"Dad kind of oversees everything. When Gideon marries, Dad'll move to a small house on the other side of the ranch, and he and Mom will probably travel."

Tiffani nodded. "Did your grandparents do that?"

"Yup. It's always worked out that way for my family. The youngest son inherits the family business. The brothers sometimes help him run it, but it's up to that generation. Dad's brothers were never interested, so it was all him and Mom. I think we'll all be involved until the day we die." Adam shrugged. "I feel like it's my calling to work with the troubled youths at the ranch."

"I love that you're doing what's right by those boys."

"It's really the only life I've ever known. You really need to meet Kevin sometime. He's a minister, and he serves a congregation in Idaho at this huge resort ranch. River's End Ranch or something like that. Maybe we can go there on our honeymoon." He didn't look at her as he said honeymoon, knowing that she would roll her eyes or complain.

"There can't be a honeymoon until there's a wedding. There can't be a wedding until there's a proposal. All I hear are assumptions that I'm going to marry you. No one has mentioned a proposal at all." Tiffani looked out the window away from him, trying to hide her grin. She knew she'd shocked him even without being an empath.

"Does that mean it's time for me to ask?"

She shrugged. "I think it's almost a foregone conclusion we'll marry. At least for you it is."

"I'll think on it." He kept driving, but his heart felt as if it was beating a mile a minute. She was willing to consider marrying him. He hadn't thought it would ever happen. Of course, he'd known her less than two weeks, but it still felt like it would never happen.

When they got to San Antonio, they returned the truck to her uncle and picked up her car, no worse for wear. It was an old, beat-up Ford Fiesta that she'd been driving since she'd gotten her license. It wasn't worth much, but it still ran well, and that's all she'd ever cared about.

He looked at it for a moment. "I don't know how I feel about you driving this thing."

She got behind the wheel and started the car. "It doesn't really matter how you feel. What matters is the car is mine."

He got into the passenger seat, scooting it all the way back. "I feel like a pretzel."

"Are you sure? Have you ever really *been* a pretzel to know what it feels like?"

"I have an imagination. And maybe I'm empathetic with random snack foods. You don't know!"

"If you're empathetic with snack foods, I cannot be seen in public with you. I have a rep to protect!"

He shook his head at her. "Just drive me to meet your mother, please!"

She picked up her phone to call her mother first. "Hey, Mom. We're heading your way from Uncle Simon's place!"

"I didn't feel like cooking. Why don't you meet me at that little Mexican place around the corner from me? You brought your Adam?" her mom asked.

Tiffani blushed, glancing at Adam to see if he'd heard. He grinned at her in a way that told her he'd not only heard, he'd liked it. "Yes, I brought my Adam. He brought me actually. I was tired this morning, so he offered to drive."

"Out late?"

"The ranch does a cookout every Friday night. We went together and stayed out until it was over. There were s'mores and everything." Tiffani knew that her mother loved anything chocolate as much as she did.

"I should have been there!"

"I sure wish you were closer." Her mother had been a cafeteria lady for the San Antonio school district for as long as she could remember.

"I do, too. We'll see each other often, though. An hour and a half is an easy drive."

Tiffani sighed. "For me." Her mother hadn't driven in her lifetime. She had always used public transportation.

"All right. I think we can be at the restaurant in twenty. Does that work for you?"

"It does. I'll see you and your Adam then."

Tiffani looked over at Adam, who was openly grinning at her. "I'm your Adam, huh?"

"I never said that. My mom did."

"Well, I like it. I want to be yours."

"We're going out for Mexican," she told him in a desperate attempt to change the subject. "I know you like Taco Bueno, but do you like other Mexican?" His mother had made Mexican for them, but she *needed* to get him talking about something else.

"I'm a Texas boy. I have Tex-Mex running through my veins."

She laughed, shaking her head as she pulled out onto the street.

When they arrived, her mother was standing outside the entrance of the restaurant, waiting for them. After Tiffani parked, she hurried to hug her mother. It had only been a week since she'd seen her, but it felt like an entire lifetime had passed. "Mom, this is Adam McClain. He's the counselor on the ranch."

"A counselor? Didn't I tell you to hold out for a doctor?" Her mother's eyes were twinkling as she said it, making it clear she was joking.

"Well, I am a psychiatrist, Mrs. Simpson. Does that work for you?"

Mrs. Simpson laughed. "I didn't mean it! I was just kidding!"

"That's all right, Mrs. Simpson. I know we're meant to be together, so nothing you say can dissuade me." Adam reached over to take Tiffani's hand in his.

"You know that after two weeks' acquaintance? You move awfully fast, Adam."

He shrugged. "What can I say? I saw what I needed and I grabbed it. It's only smart!"

"I guess so…" Mrs. Simpson looked a bit nervous after that. "Well, are we going to eat Tiffani's favorite Mexican food? She's begged to come here for every birthday since she was a little girl."

"Sounds good to me."

Tiffani led them in, a little nervous about how her mother and Adam would react to each other. They were led to a booth at the very back of the restaurant. The waitress didn't bother to ask Tiffani or her mom what they wanted. Only Adam.

"Dr. Pepper sounds good."

"I'll be right back." She hurried away, returning with ice water for Tiffani and her mother and a Dr. Pepper for Adam.

"So tell me about the ranch! I want to hear about your little house!"

Tiffani grinned, pulling her phone from her pocket. "I took pictures, because I knew you'd want to see. It's little, but it's good for me. And guess what! I got a kitten! His name is Bob."

"Bobcat? Oh, Tiffani. There are times when your sense of humor makes me wonder about you." Her mother shook her head. "It's a good thing I love you so much, and I'm not changing my mind any time soon."

Tiffani grinned, looking over at Adam who was watching her. "I love the sour cream beef enchiladas."

"Those sound good! I might try some." He barely glanced at the menu, enjoying watching her with her mother more.

Tiffani pushed her phone across the table. "Check out the photos of my little place. I finally got everything unpacked and the wall hangings up. I want to live there forever and never move."

Adam nudged her with his elbow. "It's a little small for a family."

She blushed and refused to respond. He needed to quit teasing her with her mother right there. Thankfully the waitress came back then, and she was able to give her lunch order.

When she was done, Adam shrugged. "I'll have the same thing. Sounds good."

After her mother had ordered, she pushed the phone back. "The house is very cute. I think you're really enjoying the ranch."

"I am. I have some great ideas for their big fundraiser in October of next year, and I really love living there. I'm going to nail down a taco truck this week." Tiffani leaned forward. "Do you believe the day I started the driver of the taco truck that has been coming to the ranch for the event for over ten years called to say he couldn't make it? I am not going to do this event without a taco truck!"

Her mother laughed. "If all else fails, bring me down. I'll make tacos for you."

"But that wouldn't be the same. Do you realize I've never in my life eaten a taco off a taco truck? It's like I'm deprived or something!"

"Your life is so rough. I don't know how you've lived to be twenty-eight with no tacos from a taco truck. Did you check to see if Taco Bueno has a taco truck they can send?"

Tiffani looked at her mother with shock. "I haven't! What a brilliant idea! I'll call them first thing Monday morning." She looked over at Adam. "Wouldn't it be incredible if we could get a Taco Bueno truck? I could have anything I wanted!"

"You do realize that the taco truck is for the people coming to the event and not for your personal food choices?" Adam couldn't help but tease her a little.

She shrugged. "There are some things that can be both, and the taco truck is one of them."

By the time they'd eaten, her mother was smiling. When Adam excused himself for a moment, Mom leaned forward. "You're so right. He's the right man for you. There's no doubt in my mind."

Tiffani smiled. "There's not one in mine either. He's the man for me."

"Have you told him that yet?"

"And let it go to his head? Are you kidding me?"

"What would go to my head?" Adam asked from behind her.

"You always assume we're talking about you. Adam, Adam, Adam. There are other men in this world." Tiffani slipped out of the booth and faced him. "Maybe someday you'll realize that."

"There are no other men for you." He leaned down and kissed her forehead, and she wasn't certain if she should be thrilled or embarrassed.

Turning to her mother, she asked, "Do you want us to give you a ride home?"

Her mother shook her head. "It's a beautiful day for a walk. Besides, I don't want to have to fold myself up like a pretzel in the back seat of that tin can you call a car."

Adam laughed. "Mrs. McClain, I was trying to decide if I liked you until you said that. Now I know I do. You are wonderful!"

"Call me Sharon. I can be wonderful on my own two feet." She hugged them each goodbye, whispering, "Be good!" in her daughter's ear before disappearing out the door.

"She walked?" he asked.

"Mom hasn't driven for as long as I can remember. She says she used to all the time, but I've never seen it. She is satisfied with public transportation, and I drive her where she wants to go."

"She even grocery shops that way?" He was surprised. Where he lived that just wasn't possible.

"She used to. There's this fabulous thing called grocery delivery now. She does all her shopping online and the food magically arrives. It makes her happy, and she doesn't have to have a car."

He paid for their meal, and they walked to the car together. "Do you want me to drive back?"

She shrugged. "I was planning on it, but there's a little more room in the driver's seat than any of the others. It might be best if you didn't pretzel yourself and sat there instead."

"That sounds wonderful to me!" He took the keys from her and carefully moved the seat back before even trying to sit. "Why do you drive a tin can?"

Chapter Nine

On the way back, Tiffani kept up a constant stream of chatter. She was thrilled that her mother now approved of Adam, because she was pretty sure he was what she wanted.

They were just driving onto the ranch when Adam's phone rang. He dug it out of his pocket and handed it to Tiffani. "Would you answer that for me?"

She slid her finger across the screen. "Adam's phone."

"Tiffani, this is Caleb. I think Nick is about to blow. Can you get to our cabin as fast as you can?"

"Yes, of course! We just drove back onto ranch property."

"Hurry!" Caleb sounded very concerned, which told Tiffani all she needed to know.

She hung up the phone and said, "It's Nick. Caleb wants us there ASAP."

Adam nodded, taking a side road from the main one. He drove fast, but not recklessly. When they reached the cabin, he jumped out and hurried inside, not even waiting to see if Tiffani was following him. She understood completely, wondering if she should follow. She wasn't a trained specialist in kids. She was just the woman who was coordinating their fundraiser. Their fundster.

After a moment of indecision, she followed Adam into the house, prepared to stay out of the way. What she saw when she arrived really surprised her. Every boy in the house was in the living room. Both Benjamin and Caleb were there talking to Nick, and Adam was sitting beside him on the couch, his arm around him while he cried.

Caleb walked over to where she stood and said softly, "We were in the middle of group therapy, and the other boys confronted him about not doing his share of the chores. Every new boy is eventually confronted for it, because none of them consider themselves team players. Not at first."

"So what happens now?"

"Adam will talk to him for a while. With his gift, he always knows their emotions, and he can get through in a way the rest of us can't. We'll wait for him to work his magic, but Nick has to face this in front of everyone, because he's hurting everyone with his behavior. I know it sounds strange, but it's the way we do things here."

"I think that's great," she said softly. "He should have to answer to everyone…everyone but me. I'm going to go ahead and drive home. I don't think I have any right to be here."

Caleb nodded. "We like you, but you're right. This is between his housemates and Nick."

"Tell Adam I left to go grocery shopping. I'll make something good for dinner if he wants to come over, but I'll understand if he's too busy." She took one last look at Adam, who was doing his very best to get through to the boy, and she left the house, heading for her car.

She would make a lasagna for dinner. If he wanted

some, he was welcome to come over. If he didn't, she could eat on it for a few days. She was a huge fan of leftovers, because it meant she didn't have to cook for a few days.

She picked up everything she needed for lasagna, salad, and garlic bread at the store, and then headed home. When she got there, she was surprised at how quiet it sounded. Bob came out to greet her, rubbing against her legs. She was surprised, because he usually gave her the cold shoulder when she'd been gone for a while.

At just before six, she was putting the food on the table when she heard a knock on the door. Hurrying over to answer it, she opened it wide, glad to see Adam there. He looked exhausted, as if every single ounce of energy had been drained from his body by the ordeal at the house.

She walked to him and wrapped her arms around his waist and just held on. "Are you okay?" she finally asked.

Adam nodded. "Before I got there, he was threatening suicide. When I walked in, he was ready to do it. I could feel the despair washing off him in waves. I sat with him and talked about what was expected of him here on the ranch again. I told him that each of the boys has gone through the same thing. It took hours, but we got through to him. When I left, the boys were all fixing supper together, and Nick was laughing with the others. He needed to break so he could start mending."

"Is that typical?"

"Yeah. We go through it with just about every boy who comes to live here. It's hard to deal with, because I want every one of them to be happy and fall in line, but I know it doesn't work that way." He sank onto the couch and rubbed his hands over his face, the exhaustion apparent. "But I heard my best girl was making dinner, and I couldn't not come. So are you going to feed me? Or are you going to let me sit here and starve to death?"

Adam

She laughed. "It's ready. I'll just set the table, and we can eat." She hurriedly set the table and put the salad on, bringing them plates with the rich, gooey lasagna. "I hope you like Italian."

"I'm surprised you can cook something other than Mexican. You seem to only be happy when Mexican is available to you."

She shrugged. "I like lots of food, and for some reason, I was craving lasagna tonight." She got them each a glass of water, and herself an extra glass of ice, before bowing her head for the prayer.

In his prayer, he thanked God that she was there and that they'd been in time for Nick. He asked God to watch out for the boy as well. She was touched that he was already so attached to a young man who had caused nothing but trouble in his time on the ranch. After the prayer, he ran his hands over his face, his eyes full of something she couldn't quite place.

As they ate, she talked to him about how well things seemed to have gone. "What would have happened if you hadn't been on the ranch?"

He shrugged. "They'd have held him at bay. If they're having a group session, and one of the boys tries to leave the room, they make a human wall to keep him from going. The boys have all been there, and they've done it time after time. It would have been done automatically."

"Do your brothers try to counsel if you're not there?"

"They do, but I'm rarely gone. We've never had to face this without me right in the middle of it. I feel bad that I wasn't here when it started." He shook his head, the gaze that met hers filled with pain.

She looked at him with surprise. "You think you always need to be here?"

"This ranch is my entire life. It's not just the Hippocratic Oath for me. It's that I feel the need to help each and every boy here. I know they count on me, and the state of Texas counts on me. It's not just my job. It's my everything." He ate the last bite of his lasagna and wiped off his mouth. "I've never let a woman take me away from my duties before. I think I need to reevaluate where I stand." He stood up, setting his napkin on the table. "Thanks for dinner."

He left before she could respond, leaving her staring at her empty plate. Did that mean he didn't think they were destined to marry? Exactly why did he seem angry with her? She couldn't figure him out.

She sighed, cleaning up the dishes. She wasn't about to chase after him when she had better things to do with her time.

She finished up the kitchen and walked to her living room, choosing a favorite book from her shelf. She had no desire to be around a man who didn't want to be with her.

She was even able to make out the words on the page through her tears.

———

TIFFANI SAW Adam and his entire family, along with all the boys from the ranch, at church on Sunday. Adam sat beside Nick, talking softly to him before and after the service. He never turned to look at Tiffani, and she didn't go to talk to him either. On her way out of the service, she felt a hand on her arm.

"Give him some time. He's never divided his time between work and someone he cares about before. It's always been work for him." Lillian looked at her earnestly, obviously concerned about their relationship.

"I'm going to keep working here, so he has all the time he needs to get things straight in his head."

Tiffani left the church and went home to her little house and her books. She ate leftover lasagna for lunch and took a good long nap. Her favorite thing about Sundays were the naps. Why a Sunday nap was so much better than sleeping at any other time, she didn't know, but it had always been that way for her.

She spent the entire evening listening for a knock on the door as she played with the kitten, read, and made some meals for the week coming up. She preferred to take her own cooking for lunches to work rather than go out as she had been. Of course, if she did take her lunches that would mean she'd have to give up her daily Taco Bueno, and no one wanted that.

When she went to bed, she was sad. He hadn't come by or even tried to talk to her at church. Maybe he was moving on and deciding he wanted nothing more to do with her. As she closed her eyes, she saw his face in front of her, filled with the anguish he'd shown the night before. She prayed that he'd make a decision soon, because she didn't want to be left hanging for the rest of her life.

ADAM SPENT Sunday walking the ranch. It was his home and his heritage, and he'd let a woman come between him and his work. How could he reconcile not being on the ranch when he was needed?

As he continued to walk, he sensed someone beside him. Glancing over, he realized it was his father. "Hey, Dad."

"Adam."

"What are you doing out here?"

His father shrugged. "Your mother said you were upset and walking. She said you needed me to walk with you so you could get your head on straight."

"Mom is the right woman for you. There's no doubt in my mind."

"There isn't in mine either. I knew the moment I met her I was meant to marry her, just like I know you're meant to marry Tiffani."

Adam sighed. "If I marry, Tiffani should be the one. Maybe I'm the McClain who needs to stay single."

"Why would that be true? You've heard all the family lore about how we are stronger when we're with the woman who completes us. It's true for you, just like it's true for every other man in our family." When Adam said nothing, his father continued. "What exactly happened yesterday that you're feeling so guilty about?"

Adam frowned, stopping and looking at the ground for a moment before he continued walking. "I had the best day of my life. I spent the day with the woman I care about most. I went to San Antonio with her, and we had lunch with her mother, who liked me. It was such a wonderful day. I don't think I thought of the boys more than once or twice."

"So what you're feeling guilty for is not really being gone when Nick was ready to have his breakdown, but that you weren't thinking about the boys while you were gone? That's ridiculous. When I started dating your mother, there was a new boy here on the ranch as well. You know as well as I do that there will always be a new boy on the ranch. It's the nature of what we do here. But I chose to leave that boy, who was in my house, and I went to San Antonio with your mom. We walked on the River Walk, took the boat tour of the river, and we even went to the mall there. It was truly a glorious day for me, because it's the day I realized she loved me."

"I don't know what's bad about that. You and Mom are meant to be together."

"That's right. But what I didn't tell you is that while I was gone, the new boy—his name was James—got ahold of a bottle of Tylenol. That was before we locked up the over-the-counter drugs. And he took every single pill in the bottle. By the time I got home, he was already home from the hospital. They'd had to pump his stomach. He was all right, but it could have been so much worse. We didn't have a staff psychiatrist then, just a counselor." His father shook his head. "I felt like it was my fault. I was the one James had always connected with best. If I'd only been there to keep an eye on him. If I'd only realized that he was having suicidal thoughts. If only I'd not been so wrapped up in your mother that I abandoned him for a whole day…"

"What did you do?"

"I went to James and apologized. I told him no woman would ever come before my responsibilities again. I told him that from then on I would put him before any woman."

"So you stopped dating Mom?"

His dad shrugged. "For a week or two while I got my head back on straight. James came and saw me a year or two ago. He's got a wife and four kids now. He's as happy as a clam. He told me that realizing that I would give up the woman who I was obviously meant to be with made him know he was important to someone in the world. He thought I was dumb as dirt for doing it, and he was thrilled when we started seeing each other again. But he never blamed me for what he did. As much as I thought he should have, he didn't. I don't think you should blame yourself, either."

"I don't know. Nick looked at me when I walked in there like I'd slapped him in the face. I was the one he connected with when he first got here. I'm still the one he connects the best with. I need to wait until he's more acclimated before I try to start a relationship."

"Son, there's always going to be another boy with problems. That's what this ranch is all about. If you give up the only woman you'll ever have a chance of being truly happy with for your job, you're a fool. Give Nick a week or two to settle in, and then let your lady know you love her."

"How do you know I love her?" Adam was surprised. He'd only realized himself the day before.

"Because you feel it would be a sacrifice. You're punishing yourself for not being here by giving her up. That means that you love her. I know you."

Adam sighed. "You're right. I do love her. I never thought I'd meet a woman I would want to spend the rest of my life with, and I met her, and haven't been able to think of anyone or anything. I almost couldn't figure out what to say when I got to the house last night. I let my training take over. I used my empathy. But for a minute there, I couldn't remember what to do. I felt like the worst man alive."

"I know. I felt the same way when I was in your position. Make sure Nick is good, but know that you'll never again be happy without Tiffani at your side. You might as well cut off your right arm as let her go." Patting Adam on the shoulder, his dad turned back toward the house, walking in his slow methodical way.

Adam watched him go for a moment before he resumed his walk. He wasn't ready to go back to Tiffani and beg her forgiveness, but he knew it needed to happen for them to get past this. He was in the wrong, not her. And he'd blamed her for distracting him. He had no right.

He sighed heavily. Apologizing had never been his favorite thing to do. Maybe, though, he could give it a few days before he went crawling on his knees with an engagement ring in his hand. He loved her, and he couldn't let her go.

As he kept walking, a plan began to form in his mind. He could give her time to get over the way he'd treated her as he put the plan in place. Maybe he could get his act together and make it happen. If he couldn't, he wasn't worthy of her anyway.

He had a spring in his step as he turned and headed back toward the main house. The weekend had been an eye-opening one, and he was determined that he would keep his eyes open rather than closing them again.

He showered and got ready for bed, determined he was going to treat her as any other employee for a few days until he was ready to declare his love and ask her to spend the rest of her life with him.

Once he was in bed, he folded his hands behind his head, and stared up at the ceiling. He had too much planning to do to be able to sleep. He was in love, and it was about time his lady knew about it.

Chapter Ten

At work on Monday morning, Tiffani did her best to avoid Adam. He nodded to her as he would any co-worker and went into his office, doing paperwork. She held back the tears she wanted to cry when he didn't seek her out, understanding then that it was over between them —for good.

By the time lunch rolled around, she had gotten a firm commitment from a taco truck, talked to several other vendors, and met with Lillian about the quilts she wanted to raffle off at the event. She was just hanging up the phone from talking to Kevin Roberts, a former boy from the ranch who was now a pastor. His story was different than the other boys of the ranch, but he was still a success story.

Tiffani had brought her own lunch, so she decided to just slip into the kitchen, nuke it, and get right back to work. Working lunches were nothing new to her, and they sometimes kept her from dealing with difficult things in real life. Work was good for more things than just making money.

Adam

In the kitchen, she saw Adam whispering with Brittany, and she wanted to run away and cry. The idea of him even speaking to another woman when he was angry with her broke her heart into a million tiny pieces.

When he spotted her, he nodded, then took Brittany's arm, pulling her from the kitchen to finish their conversation.

Tiffany tried not to let it bother her as she microwaved the casserole she'd made for her lunch before slipping back into her office. She needed to stay in her office or walk on the grounds of the ranch. Anywhere she couldn't see Adam and Brittany cozying up to one another.

She worked while she ate, trying to come up with new ideas to make the next year's fundraiser one that would knock people's socks off. Pony rides were a must, and they had what they needed for that. She shot off an email to Ephraim to ask if they could do hayrides every night for five dollars a head. Anything she could do to get a little extra money into the boys' pockets, she would do.

Seeing Tiffany enter the kitchen, Adam grabbed Brittany's arm and pulled her out so they could continue their conversation. Brittany had felt very much like a little sister to him since she'd started working at the ranch.

"Do you think you can have that all in place for the cookout Friday night?"

Brittany nodded, a grin splitting her face. "I love that you trust me enough to help with this. I couldn't be happier to do it!"

Adam grinned, patting her on the shoulder. "Good. I'll get her there, but you need to have everything ready for me."

Brittany saluted cheekily. "I'm here to do your bidding, boss man!"

He shook his head at her as he hurried back to his office. If Tiffany saw him whispering with Brittany, she was sure to figure out what was going on. He wanted it to be a surprise.

―――

Tiffany walked home from work that afternoon, breathing deeply as she remembered what it was she'd loved about the ranch. Somehow Adam's new attitude colored how she felt about it, and she couldn't continue to let that happen. When she got home, she opened the door for Bob to join her, and she held him on her lap as she sat on the front porch, stroking his fur. Since coming to the ranch, she'd felt like she was a part of something huge and special. Suddenly, she felt completely alone instead. At least she had Bob beside her.

When she went back inside for the night, she ate a simple supper and read for a while. She needed to find a girlfriend to hang out with there on the ranch, but the only female she'd really met was Brittany…and that was a no for now. Last week, she'd thought they'd make great friends. This week? Not so much.

As she fell asleep with Bob curled around her head, she felt a tear drip down her face and onto her pillow. She definitely felt like her world was ending. How did women go through multiple relationships and breakups?

―――

During breakfast Tuesday morning, Adam asked his dad for Tiffani's job application. He found Sharon's number and put it into his phone so he could call her from work.

"Mom, would you be willing to drive to San Antonio on Friday? There's someone I want here for the cookout."

"How am I going to get the food ready for the cookout if I'm driving an hour and a half each way? You should go."

"If I can get Brittany to help make food, will you go yourself?" Adam really wanted their two mothers to get together so they could learn about each other.

She frowned at him. "Why can't Brittany go?"

He sighed. "I guess she can. Will you accept help from Tiffani's mom with cooking if I can get her here on Thursday evening?"

She looked at him for a moment. "Tiffani's mom? Why are you bringing her here?"

"So she's here when I propose to Tiffani."

She squealed and clapped her hands. "This Friday? She thinks you hate her, you know."

"I know." He frowned. "I should probably talk to her and let her know everything is okay, but I want the proposal to be a huge surprise."

"Son, she's not going to say yes if she thinks you hate her. Sit her down and tell her that you're sorry for the way you acted, and then things will be better."

"Are you sure that's the right thing to do?"

"Trust me on this! Leave now so you can walk her to work and talk to her. Tell her you were a big buffoon, and that if she'll forgive you, you'll never act stupid again."

Adam nodded, drank down the last dregs of his coffee, and hurried out the front door. He all but ran across the ranch to her cabin, knocking on the door after catching his breath.

Tiffani opened the door and stood looking at him for a moment. "How can I help you, Mr. McClain?"

"It's Adam, and you know it. May I walk you to work? I want to explain."

She nodded briskly, going inside to get her lunch and meeting him on the front steps. "What do you want to talk about?" She fell into step beside him, making sure to keep a foot or two between them. When he touched her, her heart lost its resolve to keep him at arm's length. Her head had to stay in control.

"My entire life I've known it would be my job to help run this ranch one day. I knew I was going to be someone who counseled the boys and helped them every day. I knew it would be my whole world." He looked over at her to see how she was reacting, but she was staring straight ahead. "When my dad told me a little over a month ago that I would be meeting the woman I was destined to marry, I didn't believe him at first. And then I met you, and I knew he was right. You are my ideal woman. You care about the things I care about. You're a good person through and through." He sucked in a breath. "And then I had a boy in crisis while I was out with you, and I blew it. I knew I was hurting you and I did it anyway, telling myself I was doing what was right for the boys, who had to be my first priority."

"And now?" Was he saying he was wrong? *Please let him admit he'd been wrong.*

"Well, I acted like a big buffoon, and I promise, if you'll forgive me, I'll never act stupid again. Well, I'll *try* not to act stupid, but sometimes it's hard not to, because I have no experience with relationships. None at all." He could feel the hope radiating off of her, when before all he'd felt was pain and sadness. Was she going to forgive him?

"And what do I get to do to you if you do act like a big buffoon again?" she asked, trying not to grin. That was some apology.

"You get to...umm...I don't know!"

"Can I make you wear a baboon suit and sing and dance for the boys?"

He groaned. "You just want me to agree because you know eventually, I'm going to be stupid again."

"Well, yeah!" She closed the distance between them and slipped her hand into his. "Does this mean we're dating again?"

"If you'll forgive me and take me back." He shrugged. "I wouldn't blame you if you didn't. My own mother has been angry with me about this whole thing."

"I knew I liked your mother." They reached the office and she smiled. "I can't go through this often, but if it's a one-time thing, I can forgive and forget."

"I promise you, it's not going to happen again. I can't promise I'll be perfect, because that's not possible, but this will not happen again." He opened the door for the office and let her precede him inside. "Lunch?"

She nodded. "I brought my own, though."

"Then I'll pick something up and eat with you in the kitchen." He'd get her a taco while he was out, too. He knew her well enough to know that tacos were a necessary part of her life.

On Wednesday afternoon, Tiffani stepped out into the admin assistant's area of the office and looked around for Brittany. She had a couple of calls she needed the other woman to make for her. When she didn't see her, she walked back to Adam's office, standing in the doorway and just watching him work for a moment.

When he glanced up, his face softened as he looked at her. "What are you doing?" he asked.

"Looking for Brittany, but since I didn't find her, I thought I'd just watch you work."

"Brittany had an errand to run. She'll be back in the morning."

Tiffani frowned. "A four-hour errand? What kind of errand takes four hours?"

He shrugged. "There were several things she needed to do."

She didn't like how evasive he was being, but she trusted him, so she needed to let it go. "All right. I'll have her make these calls in the morning then."

"May I walk you home after work?" he asked, knowing that he would be able to hide her mother better if he was with her that night. She didn't ever just walk over to the main house, but the day her mother was staying there would be the day it happened.

"I'd like that." She disappeared into her office and got back to work. There was too much to do for her to stand around watching Adam work—no matter how much fun it was.

ON FRIDAY EVENING, she dressed in jeans, boots, and a checked button-up shirt. She was ready for the cookout early and sat down to wait for Adam to come and get her. They were starting to be seen as a couple all over the ranch, and as much as she loved it, it was still weird because he was her boss.

When he knocked, she hurried to the door. "Hey you!"

"Hi." He held his hand out for hers.

When she stepped outside, she saw Ephraim and Nick sitting in the front of a two-seater horse-drawn buggy. "We're not taking your truck?" she asked, trying to figure out what was going on.

"Not tonight. I want you to have a special time."

She frowned, but let him help her up into the buggy. She couldn't imagine having to climb up in a skirt, but she knew women had done it for hundreds of years. Once she was settled, Nick flicked the lines and drove them to the cookout.

It seemed to be an even bigger crowd than last week, though she knew it was just her perception. Arriving in a buggy made her feel out of place. She wished she knew what Adam was thinking, picking her up that way.

"What are you up to?" she finally asked, whispering the words.

"Me? I'm just taking my girl to dinner with lots of other people. Why?"

She didn't believe him, but she wasn't the one who was empathic.

Once they were stopped, he helped her down and she went over to mingle with others already there. Brittany was standing with Gideon again, and the two of them were laughing. Tiffani couldn't help but wonder if they were just friends, or if there was something more between them.

After the prayer, which was given by Adam's father, they followed the crowd to get in line for their food. She was walking through the line, accepting potato salad and baked beans, when she stopped short.

"Mom?"

Her mother laughed. "Yup. I wanted to see where you live, so Adam sent someone to come and get me."

"Why didn't you talk to me about it? That would have made more sense!"

Her mother shrugged. "I felt comfortable enough with Adam that it wasn't a problem to ask him."

Adam nudged her with his elbow. "You're holding up the line. I'm sure your mother will come over and join us when she's done serving all these people."

Tiffani got the rest of her food, but she was frowning as she walked to a picnic table. "What's going on, Adam?"

He shrugged. "I thought you'd enjoy your mother seeing where you work. She and my mom have become fast friends."

It wasn't really the answer she was looking for, but she didn't know how to get to the truth of the matter. She ate quietly, smiling as her mother joined them, and his parents as well.

One of his brothers pulled another picnic table closer, and then she realized they were in the middle of four different picnic tables all joined together. As she chatted with both of their mothers, they all ate.

When they were finished, his mother stood up. "It's time for cake!"

"No s'mores tonight?" Tiffani was immediately disappointed that her mother wouldn't have s'mores when she'd traveled to the ranch just for a Friday night cookout.

"Are you staying at my place tonight?"

Her mother nodded. "I stayed at the main house last night, and I cooked all day."

"You didn't have to work?"

"I get vacation days. Just because I never use them doesn't mean I don't get them!"

The cake was brought over to their table, and the boys carrying it started to tip it. She jumped up to keep them from dropping it—and that's when she saw the words that had been written onto the cake.

"*Tiffani, will you marry me?*"

She stared at it in disbelief for a moment before she turned to Adam. He was holding out a diamond ring to her.

Tears started flowing down her cheeks. How could he ask her in front of all these people when he knew it would make her cry? She nodded, then held out her left hand so he could slip the ring onto her finger.

Adam stood up and pulled her to him, kissing her softly while everyone cheered. Even Nick seemed excited that the two of them were getting married.

"When?" Adam asked.

"When what?"

"When will you marry me? I can't wait long. We could fly to Vegas tomorrow, or we could get married next weekend. Stupid three-day waiting period in Texas."

Tiffani laughed. "Don't you think we should at least have a short engagement? Where are we going to live?"

He shrugged. "We could live in your cabin. It's big enough for both of us. And there's room for us to build a house here on the ranch if that's what we want to do. Or we could buy land across the road, so we'd be close, but we would still have our privacy."

"You've thought about this a lot."

"I've thought about little else since the moment I laid eyes on you. I love you, Tiffani Simpson. I need you to marry me soon!"

She grinned. "Well, I have no desire to see Vegas, so let's marry next weekend." She turned to her mother. "Mom, can you make it here two weekends in a row?"

"How are you going to find a dress in a week?" Her

mother shook her head. "You should wait a little while so you can get what you need!"

"I'm marrying him next weekend. We'll figure out a dress."

Lillian rushed around the table to hug Tiffani. "Would you like to wear my dress? I know it was made in the early eighties, but we could fit it to you. Then you'd at least have a pretty white dress."

"And it would be something old and something borrowed. See, Mom? It's all working out."

Lillian linked her arm through Sharon's. "Leave it to us. We'll get this planned out as quickly as we can."

Sharon nodded. "I'll take the week off work, and we'll make it happen."

Sure their mothers had things under control, Tiffani reached out for Adam's hand. "Are you sure this is what you want?" she asked softly. "I don't want to take you away from your responsibilities."

"I'm sure, and you'll help me with my responsibilities. I know you'll be beside me, helping me every step of the way."

She nodded. "I will. I love you, Adam. I never believed it could happen so quickly, but we really are meant to be together. I can feel it."

He smiled, pulling her behind a tree to kiss her once more. "We are. And I thank God every day for bringing you into my life."

About the Author

www.kirstenandmorganna.com

Also by Kirsten Osbourne

Sign up for instant notification of all of Kirsten's New Releases
Text 'BOB' to 42828

And

For a complete list of Kirsten's works head to her website
wwww.kirstenandmorganna.com